CHRISTMAS BEACH WEDDING

CHRISTMAS BEACH
BOOK ONE

LORI WILDE

SUSAN SANDS

EDITED BY
KIMBERLY STRIPLING

ONE

Jane Lafitte stepped out into the bustle of Magazine Street, shivered in the cool December air, and lifted her face toward the late afternoon sun.

New Orleans was decorated with red ribbons and holly garlands on iron lampposts. Christmas music played nonstop from every business. And cinnamon brooms were everywhere, causing Jane to sneeze.

Nothing more festive than Christmastime in the Big Easy.

She had a successful meeting with the European antique supplier. Yay! It was a relief since many of their affluent clients clamored for French and English furniture for their homes. Authentic furnishings and artwork were in high demand in the home renovation business.

Jane kept an eye on the sidewalk to avoid tripping over large cracks in the cement caused by overgrown tree roots as she walked to her car parked a few blocks away.

New Orleans was a lovely old lady, but she ultimately showed her wrinkles and flaws if examined closely. Ongoing maintenance was necessary to prevent the city from falling into the Mississippi River and to preserve its beauty and history. Jane was thrilled to be a part of her city's preservation efforts, no matter how challenging.

Jane and her longtime best friend Suzy owned J&S Interiors and Renovations. Their business was based out of Suzy's home on Constantinople Street, which was a short distance from Jane's house on Napoleon Avenue.

They'd met in middle school at McGehees and

were as close as sisters, which meant they both agreed and disagreed regularly.

Today, Suzy had a conflict and couldn't make the meeting, so Jane went instead. Usually, décor and furniture were Suzy's specialty, and Jane's was renovation.

She texted Suzy the good news, and Suzy texted back with nine ladies dancing emojis, and then she added a champagne popping gif for good measure.

Yes, life was good.

Jane stopped to pick up a small Crab Louis salad she'd ordered ahead of time from a little dive place down the street. Some of the best food came from the most modest of establishments in Louisiana. The uptown afternoon traffic moved at its usual agonizing pace. She wove through the tree-lined streets for several blocks until she arrived home.

She got out of her car and inhaled deeply the pine-scented fragrance riding the breeze. Santa waved at her from the rooftop of her neighbor's house and "Santa Claus is Coming to Town" played faintly from somewhere down the block.

This was her favorite time of the year, and she was especially happy today.

Grinning, she carried her purse, mail, and take-out bag of Crab Louis up the driveway. At the back door, her gaze fell on her dormant gardenia bush and her heart tugged.

Her late husband, David, had planted the bush a year before his passing, and he'd tended it like a third child. Jane continued the loving care, and last summer, the shrub rewarded her with fragrant white blooms. David would have been so proud.

She sighed softly. She missed him so much. He'd left hole in her life she feared would never be filled.

The day after Thanksgiving, she'd hired a company to install her outdoor Christmas décor, including icicle lights, and her house looked like something from a movie set. There were wreaths on every window sporting big red bows.

Of course, it was all tastefully done. She and David had hired the firefighter-run company every year to do the decorating for them and she continued the tradition for her children. Even though her kids were young adults, they still appreciated the stability in the wake of their father's death.

Tucking away the precious memories, Jane unlocked the door just as her phone buzzed in her pocket.

She stepped inside, dropped her dinner and the mail on the kitchen counter, then hung her purse and keys beside the door. She took out her phone and was surprised to see the caller was her daughter.

It was unusual for Casey to call instead of text. Her daughter was finishing her degree in library science at Louisiana Tech in Ruston, and Casey typically only called for something important, but they did text several times a week.

"Hey, honey. How are you?"

"Hi, Mom." Casey sounded breathless.

Something was up.

Jane waited, kicking off her high heels and sinking down onto a barstool, the glow from her enjoyable day ebbing as worry crept in. Was something wrong?

"Well?" Casey asked.

Jane frowned, puzzled by the one-word question. "Well, what?"

"What do you think of Drew?"

It took Jane a second to realize Casey was following up on the selfie she'd texted to Jane earlier in the day. In the snapshot, her daughter's lovely face was squeezed next to a handsome blond man with huge blue eyes and a great smile.

The new boyfriend.

Her daughter had been dating Drew for most of the semester, but Jane had yet to meet him. Although she had seen a couple of other photos of the two of them on Casey's social media feeds. The truth was, Casey liked boys—a lot—and she had epic crushes. Jane loved her daughter dearly, but for that reason, she didn't get overly invested in every guy that Casey dated.

"He's super cute, honey." Jane didn't ask too many questions. She'd learned not to insert herself in her children's love lives. They were adults and could make their own decisions.

"OMG, Mom!" Casey exhaled in a loud whoosh. "Drew is *magnificent*. He's The One. I'm sure of it."

"I've heard that before—"

"No, I was an idiot before. I had no idea it could be like *this*. Drew is different from all the rest. You'll see."

"It's okay to take things slowly. I don't want to see you get your heart broken again."

Jane crossed her fingers and looked heavenward. *Please.*

"Mom, we *have* been taking it slowly. We've been dating since August."

Four months. The longest romantic relationship Casey had ever had. Hmm. Maybe Drew did have staying power.

"I'd love to meet him—if you think it's time for

that." Jane didn't want to meet the young man only for Casey to kick him to the curb a week later.

"We're coming home this weekend. Is that okay?"

Wow. Her heart gave a happy squeeze. Young people in the house again, yay! But that meant she had a lot of prep work to do.

"That's wonderful, sweetheart. I've missed you so much. Yes, yes, please do come home."

"I'll call Jason and ask him to be here this weekend, too."

"It's a long way to travel from Ole Miss, and final exams are harder on underclassmen than on seniors. Don't pressure your little brother to come home if he's got other plans."

"He doesn't. I texted him yesterday."

"Y'all will both be here for Christmas in a few weeks, and you were just here for Thanksgiving. It is a three-hour drive for your brother, give or take, depending on traffic."

"I know, but I want him to meet Drew, too. Oh, and tell Aunt Suzy to stop by as well."

Casey must really be serious about this boy if she wanted everyone to meet him and couldn't wait until Christmas break.

"Okay, I'll let your godmother know, and I'll have the rooms ready," she said.

"Um, Mom..."

The way she said it tapped the brakes on Jane's excitement. "Yes?"

"There's one more thing."

"What's that?"

"Drew's dad is coming to New Orleans and I... we...were hoping he could stay at your house this weekend. You know, just to have everyone close by."

Hmm, something was definitely up. She thought of the downstairs suite she only used for company. Questions buzzed through Jane's mind, but she stopped them at her teeth.

Why only his dad and not his mother? Where is he from? Is he gluten intolerant? Vegan? Keto?

Jane controlled her curiosity, knowing she would find out everything soon enough. "Alright. Where is he coming from?"

"He lives in Lafayette, but he often does consulting work in New Orleans. He's a doctor. Just so you know, Drew's mom died a couple of years ago, so don't ask about her, okay?"

That was two of her questions answered. "I'm so sorry about Drew's mom, honey. I'm sad that the two of you have that in common."

"Yeah, it's been nice for us to talk about it. Still hard, though."

"Of course it is." Jane was surprised that her daughter hadn't mentioned Drew losing his mother before. Casey had taken her dad's death very hard—they all had. "I promise not to say anything awkward to Drew or his father."

"Drew wants his dad to be there because they were supposed to go fishing at Christmas Beach this weekend, and he feels guilty about canceling on him. Plus, Drew really wants me to meet him."

Jane squashed her anxiety over having a man she'd never met sleeping in her home. She had plenty of empathy for Drew's dad and the kids, who'd both had a parent taken from them at a youthful age. Not to mention, it would be easier to have them all under the same roof.

"Is there anything else I need to know about Drew's father?" she asked.

"Hmm. Nothing that I can think of. I haven't met him yet either."

Lafayette was two and a half hours from New Orleans, so Jane could see why Drew's dad might want to stay the night—or even the entire weekend.

"You'll meet him Friday afternoon," Casey said. "He'll want to beat the traffic on I-10, so he'll probably be there a couple of hours before us because I have a test."

Jane frowned. She'd had few guests in recent years, other than the kids' college friends during carnival season. She wasn't really up for entertaining a stranger by herself, even if it was Drew's dad.

"This is really sudden, maybe he could get a hotel—"

"Gotta run. See you Friday night, Mom. Love you." With that, Casey ended the call.

✸✷✸✹✸✺✸✻✸✼✸

Dr. Trevor Gardner drove his old blue Ford pickup truck across the Bonnet Carré Spillway. He'd owned the truck since he was a teenager and he'd retrofitted it with new tech upgrades like a hands-free phone, GPS, media screen, and backup camera.

He was singing at the top of his lungs along with Faith Hill's, "This Kiss," and remembering 1998 when the song first came out...

And *poof,* his mind flooded with thoughts of his first love.

Jane Theriot.

He saw her as she'd been—perky, cute as a speckled pup—flashing him a wide grin. Giving a saucy shake of her head, blond ponytail bouncing as she playfully stuck her tongue out at him from the passenger seat of this very truck and batted her gorgeous green eyes. The memory of her taste flooded his mouth as surely as it had when he kissed her to this song.

Unexpected blast from the past. Songs were time machines, whisking people back to the first time they heard them. Jane Theriot. The one who got away.

Trevor hadn't thought about Jane in years. Hmm, wonder what she was up to? Married, most likely. Kids for sure. She'd always wanted children. They both had.

His cell phone rang. It was his son.

Drew was in his senior year at Louisiana Tech in Ruston, working on his architectural engineering degree. Tech was nearly three hours north of their home in Lafayette, and it had been a long four years. Drew came home every other month, or Trevor shot up there for a quick weekend. Still, being apart was tough, especially after losing Laura.

Trevor turned off the Faith Hill song and answered the phone through his hands-free device. "Hey there, bud. What's up?"

"Hi, Dad. I just wanted to check in with you and Henry."

"If I didn't know better, I'd think you liked that old hound dog better than you do me." Trevor chuckled.

"Of course I do," Drew teased. "Henry doesn't ask me about my grades."

"Henry doesn't pay your tuition either. How *are* the grades?"

"Walked right into that, didn't I." Drew laughed. "Relax, Dad, I'm carrying a 3.9 GPA this semester."

"Hot dog, Drew, that's awesome news. Congrats!"

"How *is* Henry?"

"Fine. He's at Juju's house." Julie, or Aunt Juju, was Trevor's deceased wife's sister and their closest kin besides Trevor's parents. Julie owned acreage outside Lafayette. "I've got too many consults this week to bring him with me."

"For sure, he's better off at the farm while you're in New Orleans," Drew said. "Henry does love those farm goats."

"So, is everything all right?" Trevor asked. "We still heading to Christmas Beach this weekend?"

"Um... everything's okay. I just missed you and Aunt JuJu and Henry."

Trevor heard a hitch in Drew's voice. "But...?"

"How do you know there's a 'but'?"

"Drew, I'm your *faw*-ther," he said, affecting a Darth Vader accent. "I know you. What's on your mind?"

"Would it be okay if we postponed the fishing trip until Christmas break? There's someone I want you to meet."

"What's her name?"

Drew's tone lit up. "Her name is Casey, and she grew up in New Orleans.."

Huh. So Drew had a serious girlfriend. Trevor tried not to press for more information, but his curiosity yammered at him. His son hadn't *ever* brought a girl home before. Who was she? How long had they been going out? Where did they meet?

"Dad?"

"Yeah?"

"I think she's The One." A dreamy quality infiltrated Drew's voice.

Two conflicting emotions hit Trevor at once. Excitement for his son and dread fear that he'd get hurt. Drew was levelheaded, but Trevor had been too, until Jane Theriot had done a number on his heart.

No, it wasn't fair to paint Drew's girlfriend with

the Jane Theriot brush. Just because Trevor's first serious romance blew up in his face, didn't mean that would happen to Drew.

"I'll send you her pic."

"That's fantastic, Bud. I can't wait to meet her. Send me the details of when and where we're meeting."

"Will do."

They ended the call, and he got two texts from Drew as he pulled over for fuel. Pumping gas, he took out his phone. The first text was of a sparkly green-eyed brunette with a deep dimple in her right cheek. He could see why his son was smitten. That dimple reminded him of a girl he'd known decades ago.

Jane Theriot.

What was with him today? Why was he thinking so much about Janie? He hadn't seen the woman in over twenty-five years. He blamed Faith Hill. Her song had stirred up the past. For half a second, he was tempted to google Jane and see what was going on in her life, but that felt desperate somehow.

The pump clicked off. Trevor rehoused the nozzle, got in his truck, and drove away, still seeing Janie in his mind's eye, the dimple dug deep in her cheek, her laughing green eyes trained on his as she went up on tiptoe and stole a kiss. The woman had been so full of life, and he'd once loved her so very much.

But the past was the past. No amount of wishing and hoping could roll back the clock. And really, he wouldn't do it if he could. Laura had been an amazing wife and gifted him with his precious son. He didn't regret any of it.

Besides, it was Drew's time. This was his son's first love, not Trevor's, and he would support Drew any way he could.

Determined to empty his head of useless nostalgia, Trevor tuned his satellite radio to the holiday music channel and sang Christmas songs all the way home.

Two

On Friday, Jane took the afternoon off work and triple-checked her list to make sure she'd done everything before her guests arrived.

Food stocked. Check. House spic-and-span, thanks to her longtime housekeeper, Doris, who'd just left. Check. Flowers in the bedrooms. Check. Fresh towels in the bathrooms. Check. Clean linens on the beds. Check. Scented candles lighted to make the house feel inviting. Check. Christmas music playlist created. Check.

She was ready for guests.

Drew's dad should be there in about ninety minutes. Honestly, she was a bit nervous about spending time alone with a man she did not know.

There was only one last chore before she hopped in the shower and dressed for company. Barefooted and in her oldest pair of jeans with holes in the knees and wearing a lightweight pale-yellow sweatshirt, she padded outside to water the plants.

New Orleans rarely grew cold until January, and this afternoon, the temperature was in the low sixties.

Casey hadn't mentioned Drew's dad's name, or maybe she had and Jane had simply forgotten it. She blamed her memory slip on having just turned fifty last month. Hard to believe, especially since Jane still felt fresh out of college some days, although on other days, not so much.

After she finished soaking all the Boston ferns hanging from the iron hooks that David had installed a decade ago across the front porch, she moved the hose to the Christmas tree-shaped topiaries. They were planted in pots that flanked both sides of the front door and were filled with purple pansies.

The crunch of vehicle tires on her white shell driveway drew her attention to a light-blue vintage Ford pickup truck pulling in.

A strange sensation of déjà vu washed over her, but she pushed the feeling aside. Jane was not a fanciful person. Yes, she'd once known a handsome boy who drove such a truck, but that was a long time ago.

This must be Drew's father arriving earlier than expected.

Great. She was dressed like a vagabond. Jane looked down and saw a dirt smudge on her shirt and tried to brush it away, but it simply smelled. So much for first impressions.

Oh, well.

She squared her shoulders, pasted on a welcoming smile on her face, and waved like she was thrilled to see him.

Jane couldn't make out his face through the glare on the truck's tinted windows. She could only see that he wore sunglasses and a cowboy hat. She motioned him toward the back of the house, where the driveway led to a parking pad alongside her garage.

He got the message and pulled forward.

Still barefooted, Jane trailed after him, admiring the old truck. It did look remarkably similar to the one her old boyfriend drove. Same color, same make, same model.

Trevor Gardner.

The name floated into her mind. Where was he now?

When they dated, he was pre-med and excited about becoming a doctor. Had he achieved his dreams? She hoped so. Despite their bad breakup, she had wanted only the best for him. He'd been a good man. They just wanted different things and circumstances had torn them asunder.

Over the years, she'd thought of Trevor from time to time, especially after David had died, but she resisted looking him up on social media. The past belonged in the past and besides, the man was no doubt happily married with a passel of adorable children. She'd always known Trevor would make the cutest babies.

Not that she was jealous. She had a couple of gorgeous babies of her own. No regrets. Things had turned out the way they were supposed to. David had been a devoted husband and father, and they'd had twenty-one wonderful years together. Greedily, she'd wanted more, but the hand of fate had dealt her different cards.

The pickup truck parked, and the engine shut off.

Jane walked closer.

The driver's door opened and the first thing she saw was a pair of cowboy boots, followed by long legs in crisply starched Wrangler jeans, and then the lanky man in a cowboy hat and sunglasses stood in her driveway. He turned to look at her.

Jane's heart fluttered, and she completely lost her breath.

No, it simply couldn't be!

Not with a big welcoming grin on his face. Not the last person in the world she ever expected to see today, or ever again, frankly.

Twenty-five years older, but more handsome than ever. The man who'd once been the love of her life.

Trevor Gardner.

❋❋❋❋❋❋❋❋❋❋

Trevor's first impression when he pulled up to

the Napoleon Avenue, raised Center Hall Cottage style house, pale-gray with white shutters and porches running across both upstairs and down, was plush, elegant, and yet homey. Casey's family had a lovely place in a stately neighborhood with a rich history.

Color him impressed.

When he first turned into the driveway, the sun had been in his eyes and despite his sunglasses, he'd almost missed seeing the lithe woman around his own age standing on the front porch and pointing him toward the rear of the house.

Following her instructions, he'd eased past the big fenced backyard with a giant oak tree. Good place for Henry to run around.

Whew. He was glad. Because his sister-in-law, Julie, hadn't been able to take his hound dog this weekend as planned, so he'd been forced to bring Henry along. He hoped Casey's folks didn't mind the imposition.

Already feeling a little intimidated, he parked on the pad. He killed the engine and stepped from the truck.

He turned to see the woman, who was now standing behind his truck, hands on her hips, watching him. He got a good look at her for the first time. She was silhouetted by the late afternoon sun falling across her golden hair. Instantly, his heart skipped a beat and his skin flushed hot as he recognized her.

No.

It couldn't be.

Time warped, and he blinked hard. He *had* to be seeing things.

But the slender blonde standing barefoot on the concrete was still there. No mirage. Strangely, it was the woman who'd lately been on his mind, as if life was playing a cosmic joke on him.

Jane Theriot.

Trevor felt his jaw go slack as the realization hit him in waves. His son's girlfriend's mother was none other than his first love, Jane Theriot.

What were the odds? Stunned, he could barely look away from her. She was as beautiful as ever, older, yes, but still captivating.

Jane Theriot, the one who had gotten away.

His chest tightened and his gaze flicked to her eyes. From her expression, she was just as shocked as he was. He felt a pang of familiarity, like an old song coming back to him. It had been so long since he'd seen her.

Suddenly, all the emotions that he'd hidden for

so many years came flooding back. He was overwhelmed by a sense of nostalgia and longing for what might have been. He wanted to speak, to say something, but he didn't quite know where to begin.

He cleared his throat, and the awkward sound seemed to break the spell.

Jane blinked as if snapping back to the present, just as he was.

He whipped off his sunglasses and stuck them in his shirt pocket. "J-Janie? Is that really you?"

"Trevor?" Her eyes widened, and she swayed, wobbly on her feet.

Hell, he was pretty shaky himself. He was unsure what to do, and she seemed just as uncertain.

"You're Casey's mom?" he asked.

Just as she said, "You're Drew's dad?"

"Yes," they replied in unison.

Jane's eyes widened and her face paled, and Trevor was pretty sure he looked just as dumbfounded as it sank in that their adult children were dating. He tipped back his cowboy hat and studied her. She eyeballed him just as closely.

"Do you think the kids know about us?" he asked.

"How would they? It's not as if I've ever talked to them about you."

"Ditto. I had no idea Casey was your daughter." But he'd seen those green eyes and that dimple in Casey's photo and felt a soft kick in his gut. Now he knew why Casey seemed so familiar.

"Oh, dear." Jane put a hand to her heart, and for a minute there, he thought she might faint. "This is a *total* disaster."

Total disaster? Was she still holding a grudge after all these years? Yes, he'd made a terrible mistake back then. A mistake he regretted to this day, but two and a half decades had passed. Surely her animosity toward him had ebbed somewhat.

He stepped closer, to be nearer in case he had to scoop her up before she toppled over. "Well, it's not all that bad, is it?"

"I need to sit down," she said, her voice coming out fragile and wispy. "Let's go inside."

"Before we do, there's something I need to mention."

Her jaw tightened, and the muscle at her chin ticked. She looked braced for a blow. *Aww, Janie.* Did he still stir her grief?

"What is it?" she asked in a brittle tone.

"I ran into a little hiccup as I was leaving home."

"What kind of hiccup?" She pulled her bottom

lip up between her teeth, a habit she had whenever she was uncertain. Some things didn't change.

He softened his voice and upped his smile. Trevor wanted her to know she had nothing to fear from him. "Nothing big. My sister-in-law had a small emergency and couldn't take care of Henry as planned."

"H-Henry? Who's Henry?"

Trevor pointed toward his pickup. "He's my hound dog."

"You brought a *dog*?" Her tone was flat, her expression neutral.

"Yes, but he's potty-trained and mostly well mannered."

"I like dogs, but I don't have any of my own." She was nibbling on her lip again. "Would it be possible for him to stay outside?"

"Well, he digs a little, so I wouldn't want him to get ahold of your beautiful flowers." He gestured toward her flower garden. He still couldn't get over the fact that Casey's mother was Janie Theriot.

She let out a little puff of air that stirred the hairs framing her face. "I see."

"He'll stay right by my side," Trevor said. "I promise. He's been treated for ticks and fleas, and he just had a bath. I take him to the vet regularly." Okay, he was overexplaining, trying to put her—and himself if he were honest—at ease. "I'll look after him, so you don't have to worry about a thing."

She finally offered a smile, but it seemed forced.

Trevor got it. This was a lot. Finding out your ex-fiancé was your daughter's boyfriend's dad was unsettling and then to learn he'd brought his hound dog to the weekend meet and greet; he couldn't blame for being thrown off-balance. Lord knew he was.

"Go ahead." She motioned toward his truck and her smile grew warmer. "Bring him on in."

"Thanks." He grinned. She'd always been a good sport. "I appreciate you rolling with the punches."

"Punches," she echoed.

He understood that one hundred percent. Discovering their kids were dating was a wallop to him, too. Trevor let Henry out of the truck and the hound dog immediately raced over to Jane.

Looking nervous, she backed up, clutching her hands together as her smile vanished. Henry sank down on his haunches in front of her, and then sat up straight, paws in front of him, demonstrating the begging trick Drew had taught Henry.

Jane threw Trevor a look. "What does he want?"

"Just a little scratch behind the ear."

Hesitating, Jane studied Henry for a moment, then slowly bent from the waist and leaned over to scratch Henry behind his ear.

His hound, that friendly mutt, licked Jane squarely in the face.

Jane sputtered, jumped backward, and pulled her palm down her face. "Ugh."

"Henry! No licking! I'm so sorry," he apologized.

"I'm okay." She wiped her palm on her jeans. "A little dog slobber never hurt anyone. He just took me by surprise."

Trevor grabbed Henry's collar and tugged him away from Jane. "He was actually my wife, Laura's dog. He's really affectionate, especially with women."

Jane lowered her lashes, shot him a sidelong glance, and quipped, "Reminds me of a guy I used to know."

With that, she turned and sauntered into her house.

Leaving Trevor and Henry to hustle after her. Oh boy, at this rate, it was gonna be a very long weekend indeed.

THREE

Jane stared at the one person from her past she'd thought never to see again—*hoped* never to see again.

Trevor Gardner.

With a tagalong hound dog named Henry.

The dog wagged its tail and peered at her with limpid brown eyes, as if begging her forgiveness for the face lick.

Jane wasn't so fussy as to blame the dog for being

a dog. She'd just been caught off guard, both by the dog and the stunning realization that her daughter was dating Trevor's son.

The coolness of the mudroom tile seeped through the soles of her bare feet. Gracious! She wished she'd worn shoes.

Too late now.

There was something unseemly about greeting a former lover with naked toes. It felt too intimate. But hey, at least she'd gotten a midwinter pedicure, and her toes were painted red with green Christmas trees.

Trevor glanced down at her feet, probably because she'd been staring at her toes instead of him.

"Are you okay?" he asked.

"Yes, fine." She pasted on a bright smile. "Just surprised to see you."

"Ditto."

"You haven't changed a bit," she said, finding herself engrossed in his beautiful blue eyes that were as deep as a cool mountain stream. She'd forgotten just how arresting his eyes were.

"Neither have you," he murmured, his gaze locked on her face.

Jane's pulse still revved high. She'd like to think it was because the dog licked her, but she knew it was the handsome man grinning at her as if twenty-five years hadn't flown by them in a whoosh.

"Well," she said. "Well."

Yes, why, thank you, I am a brilliant conversationalist.

"So, this is... unexpected." He stuffed his hands in his pockets, same old gesture he used whenever he was uncertain.

"Yes, *so* unexpected." And awkward. But Jane had cut her teeth on Southern hospitality. She could navigate this little pothole in life's road.

"Here, let me show you to your room so you can put your things away." She pointed to his duffel.

"Are you sure you want us to stay here? We can try to find a pet-friendly hotel nearby if this is too much of an inconvenience." His voice was richer than it had been, fuller, deeper.

"Certainly not. It's only for two nights and the kids are expecting you to stay here. You and Henry will bunk in the downstairs guest suite. Follow me. It's this way." She headed toward the short flight of stairs and led him into the airy, open space.

"You have a lovely home," he said.

The ceilings were a foot lower in the downstairs suite than in the main house, but it still gave Trevor a foot of clearance.

"Thanks. We did a complete renovation a few years ago."

We.

The word felt weighted somehow. Heavy with complexity and complications.

"You and your husband?" he asked, setting his duffel bag on the queen-sized bed's coverlet.

"Yes." She smiled softly. "David and I were married for twenty-one years. He died almost three years ago from pancreatic cancer."

"That had to be rough for you after your..." Trevor winced.

She knew what he was thinking and why he'd broken off the sentence. She let the whole thing go. She would *not* be the one to bring up Chad.

"Pancreatic cancer is difficult," he murmured. "Hard to diagnose until the disease has progressed too far for treatment to be effective."

"Yes," she said barely above a whisper.

"I'm so sorry for your loss."

The condolences from anyone else might have sounded rote, but there was sincere sympathy in Trevor's voice. He *was* sorry that she had suffered.

She pressed two fingers to her mouth and nodded. "Thank you. I understand you've been through a similar grief of your own."

"Yes, my wife Laura. We married at the end of my residency. She was a classmate, although she ended up not practicing medicine in favor of raising Drew. I lost her two years ago in a car accident." He grimaced.

Empathy for this man tugged at her heart. "It is tough. I hate that we have this terrible thing in common."

"Yeah." His gaze held hers. "Drew and I are still working through the loss. Holidays are the worst."

"Yes, they are."

A long silence passed between them. A moment for their departed spouses.

"I'm glad you had a good life with Laura," she said. "You deserved it."

He nodded. "I feel the same for you and David."

She blinked away the mist in her eyes and added a cheery tone to her voice. "The bathroom's through here. There are fresh towels and washcloths. Let me know if you have any burned-out lightbulbs." She knocked on the doorframe. "Old house. The light-bulbs go out often."

"Thanks again for having us. I know I'm the last person you expected to see today."

"Yes, you are." She hesitated, wanting to say more, but it wasn't the time or place. If their kids were serious about each other, they'd have other opportunities to chat. "Make yourself comfortable while I go change my clothes and start dinner." She moved toward the door, then paused and turned back to him. "Oh, do you have any food restrictions?"

"Nope. Drew doesn't either. We're not picky eaters, so we're good with whatever you make."

"I've got a nice merlot breathing if you want a glass."

"Thanks. I'll be up shortly, after Henry and I get settled in."

"I'll bring a bowl down for you to give him water."

"That's okay. I brought his food and water bowls with me."

"All right then." She turned for the door.

"Jane?"

She stopped and turned back. "Yes?"

"Don't change your clothes on my account. I think you look fantastic."

Jane didn't know how to respond to his words or the friendly look in his eyes, and she took a deep breath. "Since I haven't met Drew yet and Casey would die if I was wearing a ratty old sweatshirt and holey jeans when they arrive, I think I'll change."

Better get control of yourself, and quick.

If she kept having this kind of reaction to the man, it would be a very long weekend for sure.

Jane hurried upstairs, pulse still racing. Seeing Trevor again rattled her more than she cared to admit. Taking a fortifying breath, she collected herself.

Twenty-five years.

A quarter of a century since they'd been together. Since she'd love him with a passion bordering on obsession. Since she'd believed they would spend the rest of their lives together happily ever after.

Until everything had fallen apart spectacularly.

She needed to talk to someone who would understand the implications of having her first love, who'd hurt her so badly, staying underneath her roof. In her bedroom, she flopped down on her bed and took out her phone to call Suzy.

"Hey, there," Suzy said. "Why the phone call since you just sent me an epic text?"

"You don't want to hear from me?"

"I *always* want to hear from my 'ride or die.'" Suzy laughed.

Her best friend since childhood, turned business partner, had a way of making Jane feel supported and grounded. Exactly what she needed now that her world had tilted on its axis.

"I just wondered," Suzy said. "Aren't you supposed to be entertaining Casey's new boyfriend's dad?"

"I am." Jane paused, reluctant to even say the words out loud.

"It's going that badly?"

"Okay, Suzy, brace yourself, you will not believe this."

"Uh-oh. Do you need me to come over there?"

"No, no. We'll see you soon enough at dinner tomorrow night as planned. I just wanted to prepare you for what's happened."

"I'm braced. Let it fly."

"Guess who Drew's dad is?"

"I have no idea."

"Drew's last name is Gardner."

There was silence on the other end.

"Suzy?"

"*No!*" Suzy said.

"*Yes.*"

"Please don't tell me Trevor Gardner is in your guest suite."

"I'd love to be able to tell you that, but unfortunately—"

"Get him out of there!"

"I can't."

"Holy Christmas, this is unbelievable!"

"Tell me about it."

"This is complicated."

"Uh-huh."

"Omg. Trevor Gardner."

"Yeah."

"Umm, hopefully Drew will go the way of Casey's other short-lived romances and be gone before Christmas."

"I can only pray," Jane said and fell back against the pillows. But she felt badly about that because Casey really did seem serious about Drew.

"I'm stunned."

"Me too." Jane swallowed. "Want to know the worst part?"

"All ears."

"He's just as gorgeous as ever."

"Oh no, Jane. Please don't tell me you still got the *feels* for him."

"I wouldn't call it 'feels' exactly, but we never had real closure and I just, well, I've been flooded with memories."

"Yeah, well, don't forget how he left you high and dry in your time of need."

"But Suzy, this feels like the hand of fate. I mean, what are the odds?"

"Twelve thousand students attend Louisiana Tech, and your kids both went to your alma mater. I'm guessing, the odds are somewhere between twelve thousand to one, so not *really* astronomical."

"What if Trevor and I are meant—"

"No," Suzy said firmly. "I watched you grieve that man twenty-five years ago. I'm not doing it again."

"We were kids back then—"

"So don't be a middle-aged fool."

"But maybe our have paths have crossed for a reason. We're both widowed and—"

"You know, Jane, just because paths cross again, it doesn't always mean they're meant to merge. Maybe it's just a chance to acknowledge the past so you can move forward. Perhaps that's the message you're meant to receive."

"Thank you," Jane said. "For being the voice of reason."

"Got your back, always."

"I appreciate you so much."

"See you tomorrow night. Until then, take care."

"Bye."

"Love you."

"Love you, too."

Jane ended the call. Suzy was absolutely right. Just because fate had deposited Trevor at her door, it didn't mean they should rekindle things. It would be foolish. Especially since their adult children were involved with each other.

Shaking off silly hopes and dreams that she hadn't even known she'd been entertaining, Jane hurried to the bathroom to shower and change. She needed to focus on the evening ahead of her, not wallow in the past. She could handle this. She was a mature and rational adult.

Bolstered by Suzy's pep talk, she made a solid plan. For the next forty-eight hours, she'd stay as far away from Trevor as circumstances allowed.

★★★★★★★★★★★

Aware of the minefield they were navigating, Trevor came upstairs after making Henry comfy in the basement, with a chew toy and a bowl of water. He turned the TV on to Animal Planet to keep his dog company.

As he followed his nose to the kitchen, Trevor

studied the framed photos on the wall in the hallway. There was a picture of Jane with a handsome dark-haired man, who must be her late husband, beaming with their son and daughter. Jane in a white wedding dress, glowing with joy. Jane and her family on vacations, holidays, and birthdays.

Seeing glimpses of the beautiful life she built without him stirred old regrets. If only things had worked out differently between them... but no, things had happened the way they were supposed to for him. He'd built a fine life of his own with Laura and Drew. Until the worst had happened and he'd lost his beloved wife.

All he and Jane could do was move forward, for the sake of their children, and let go of the past.

He found her in the kitchen.

She wore dark well-fitting jeans paired with a navy sweater and black flat-soled ankle boots. Her hair was brushed back off her forehead in an elegant style and gold earrings glistened from her delicate earlobes.

Once upon a time, he'd enjoyed nibbling those same lobes. Before he'd met Laura, Trevor had imagined a million times what it might be like to see Jane again. A sliver of regret slid in.

Stop it.

He quelled the memory. None of that nonsense. Their kids were involved with each other. It would be a dicey enough weekend without stumbling down memory lane.

"Smells amazing." He inhaled the aroma of onions, bell pepper, and celery simmering. The holy trinity. Plus, garlic. No Cajun dish was complete without those ingredients.

Jane turned from the stove. She moved with the same grace he remembered, and she looked at ease in her kitchen, with its white subway tile, marble countertops, and shiny hardwood floors. Very nice.

"I'm making shrimp étouffée with salad and garlic bread. Nothing fancy," she drawled in her sweet Southern accent.

"Can I help with dinner?" he asked.

"I've got this under control. There's wine and glasses on the island. Help yourself." She turned halfway and pointed but didn't meet his gaze. She faced the gas range, holding a wooden spatula and stirring the Magnalite pot.

"Nice pot. I haven't seen one of those in years." The oval Magnalite cast aluminum cookware was a Louisiana classic discontinued in the nineteen-nineties.

"It was my grandmother's," she said. "I feel honored to have inherited it."

He sat on one of the barstools and reached for the merlot. "Would you like some wine?"

She held up a quarter-full glass. "Way ahead of you."

"How are your parents?" He realized this was touchy territory, but it was the polite thing to ask. Her parents had been quite upset after Jane broke up with him, but of course, they'd taken her side. He didn't blame them. Didn't blame anyone but himself.

"They're the same—older. Momma still nags Daddy daily, only now, it's about his salt intake and getting overheated while he gardens in the summer or walks the dog."

"Mine do the same thing." Trevor chuckled. "They still live here in New Orleans on the same house across the lake and worry about the next hurricane."

"We're lucky to still have our parents."

"Yes, we are." He paused and studied her as she leaned against the counter and sipped her wine. "So, do you want to talk about... this?" He toggled his finger back and forth between the two of them. "Before our kids arrive?"

"I don't, actually." She sliced him with a sharp look. "*This* is some stranger-than-fiction stuff we won't resolve by reopening that old can of worms."

Oh, okay. Message received. She didn't want to talk about it. Yet. "I was just wondering if we should tell them that—"

Just then, the back door slammed open.

He and Jane turned in unison.

"Surprise!" Casey and Drew came barreling into the kitchen.

"Yay!" Jane put down her wineglass and opened her arms wide. "Y'all are earlier than I thought you'd be."

Casey hugged her mother. "My professor rescheduled the test for Tuesday, so we left right after class." She stepped back and pulled Drew forward. "Mom, this is Drew."

"It's so nice to meet you, Drew." Jane's eyes lit up and she thrust out her hand to shake Drew's hand.

"You too, Mrs. Lafitte." Drew sniffed the air. "Something smells great."

"Shrimp étouffée. The rice is almost ready, so we'll eat soon." Jane studied his son, sizing him up.

Trevor did the same with Casey, stunned at how much she looked like her mother.

Drew came over to clap Trevor on the shoulder, and then he reached out a hand to Casey and tugged her to him. "Case, meet my dad, Trevor."

With all the manners and grace of her mother, Casey gave Trevor a charming smile and shook his hand. "Thank you for coming to visit this weekend, Mr. Gardner. We're so excited we could make it."

"I wouldn't have missed it for the world. It's great to meet you, Casey," Trevor said.

"Where's Henry?" Drew asked.

"He's in the guest suite." Trevor nodded in the direction of his accommodations.

"Wow, really?" Casey arched an eyebrow at her mother. "I can't believe you let a dog in the house, Mom." Casey turned to Trevor. "She never let us have a dog growing up."

"Really?" Trevor asked, surprised. When they were dating, Janie had adored dogs. "That doesn't sound like the Janie—"

He broke off. The kids were staring at him, and Jane was shooting him the evil eye. He'd almost inadvertently told them he and Jane had a past together. Yikes. He needed to curb his tongue.

"David was allergic to dogs," Jane said in an efficient tone, glossing right over Trevor's gaffe. "Why don't y'all bring in your luggage and get settled?

Dinner will be ready soon. I put Drew in the blue guest bedroom. Casey, do you have any idea when your brother will get here?"

"I texted Jason a couple of hours ago, and he said he was on the road." Casey waggled her cell phone. "So I expect him to be here soon. Want me to text him again?"

"He's driving, leave him be," Jane said.

"C'mon, Case." Drew motioned for her. "I'll introduce you to Henry, and then we'll unload the car." Drew and Casey headed for the downstairs guest suite, leaving Trevor and Jane alone in the kitchen again.

Their eyes met.

"We can't *not* tell them about us," Trevor said. "Sooner or later, one of us will slip up like I just did."

"I know," she said.

"We should game this out."

"Nothing to game out. Let me choose the time, place, and manner to break the news," she said.

"Okay." Trevor nodded.

Some things never changed. Same old Janie. She hadn't lost the need to be in control.

FOUR

Jane could feel Trevor's gaze boring into her back. "Stop that."

"What?"

She looked over her shoulder, caught him grinning, and shot him a chiding look. "You know."

"Alright, you caught me staring. I just can't get over how little you've changed." He shook his head and his thick hair bounced with the movement.

"Oh, you are so wrong. I'm a middle-aged

woman with two grown children, a trick knee, and a mortgage." She didn't mention how unchanged he seemed to her.

His bright-blue eyes and the deep voice that sent little darts of memories through her every time he spoke. It was silly to be so affected by the man, and yet she was.

"Looks like you're doing pretty well with it," he murmured.

Jane shrugged and sipped her wine as the food simmered. "It's been hard work keeping my head above water with two kids in college."

"I hear that, but you make the struggle look easy."

"Can you grab that bread from the oven?" She tossed a potholder his way to hide her blush at his compliment.

"Sure." He sauntered over, coming within a foot of where she was tossing the salad.

Too late, she realized her critical mistake, inviting him within the perimeter of her personal space. He was far too close. She could smell his woodsy cologne and when he bent to open the over door...

Have mercy!

Her heart skipped as she unabashedly studied the

way his jeans stretched across a backside that was as firm as it had ever been.

Memories of their passionate past flooded her mind, causing waves of nostalgia to course through her body. She hadn't seen him in twenty-five years, but the connection between them was still there, as thick and palpable as the steam rising from the pot on the stove.

He leaned in to grab the bread with the oven mitt and a shiver went straight down her spine. She stepped back, hoping he didn't notice how much he affected her.

Trevor lifted his head, and his eyes met hers. He lowered his lashes as if he was also feeling something similar. "Where should I put this?"

She couldn't answer, couldn't speak past the lump in her throat. She waved at the trivet on the counter and watched him, hyperaware of every movement he made, every glance they shared. She felt transported back in time to when they were young, when their love had been fresh and new and all-consuming...

After settling the bread pan down on the trivet, he turned back to her, an uncertain smile touching the corners of his full lips. Lips she'd once kissed. Did he still taste the same? Like lazy summer afternoons and cherry lemonade?

"Do you need anything else?" He sounded earnest, sincere, but looked as if he'd rather bolt than stay in the same room with her.

The feeling was mutual.

His eyes caught on hers. Jane didn't blink.

Neither did Trevor. It felt as if they were locked together, unable to glance away. Clearly, neither of them knew how to handle this sudden reunion after all these years apart. But fate had brought them together again. By chance, their children were dating each other now. And neither wanted to be the first to break eye contact or look away from each other's gaze.

"I—"

"Do—"

"You go first." She waved.

"No, you."

In unison, they opened their mouths to speak at once, stopped, and laughed.

"Aren't we slick?" Trevor asked.

"The smoothest."

"Sophisticated."

"Modern."

Locking eyes again, they both laughed.

"Mom," Casey called, appearing in the kitchen with Drew following close behind. She waved her phone in the air. "Jason will be here in fifteen minutes."

"Great. We can put the food on the table now. He'll be right on time."

Jane pulled out the placemats from one of the island drawers and laid them beside the short stack of shallow stone-colored bowls she'd set out earlier. They would eat family-style at the six-person kitchen table. No need to use the formal dining room.

"I'll set the table." Casey grabbed plates, placemats, and a stack of square white paper napkins.

"I'll help." Drew took the plates from her.

"Y'all get your drinks too," Jane said. "There's wine open, and the beer and soft drinks are in the fridge and water in the pitcher."

"I'll put ice in glasses," Trevor volunteered.

"Thank you," she said, keeping her voice neutral.

Jane ladled the steaming étouffée into a large shallow stoneware serving dish that would keep it warm for hours, then did the same with the cooked rice.

Trevor filled five tumblers with ice from the counter ice machine. Afterward, he grabbed the bread knife from the wooden block on the countertop and began slicing the sourdough loaf. Without speaking, they worked in tandem to get food on the table, and by the time dinner was ready, Jason's Mustang rumbled to a stop in the driveway.

Jane thought the vehicle was entirely too noisy. But Jason adored the car he and his dad had so lovingly restored. He liked to say, "As long as I have the 'stang, I've got Dad with me."

Two minutes later, Jason burst into the kitchen with a big grin on his face. Her son tackled life full force with no subtlety or hesitation. "Hey, y'all. I'm home!"

"Glad you're back, sweetheart." Jane wrapped her son in a big hug, and he lifted her off her feet, making her giggle.

Jason picked up Casey next and twirled her around a few times. She squealed with delight. "I've missed you, Goober."

"I'm not a goober. You are." Slipping her arm around her brother, Casey turned to introduce him. "Jason, this is my boyfriend, Drew, and his dad, Mr. Gardner."

They all shook hands.

"Okay, everybody hungry?" Jane motioned toward the laden table.

A chorus of yeses filled the kitchen. Jane

watched everyone taking their seats around the dining nook table. She ended up between Jason and Trevor, and directly across from Casey and Drew. Not exactly ideal positioning, given the circumstances.

Trevor shot her an uncertain look as he sat down, clearly just as uncomfortable with their proximity as she was. Jane busied herself passing around the étouffée and rice as if everything was normal.

As hostess, it was her duty to keep conversation flowing. She started with small talk about the weather and everyone's travels. Casey and Drew chatted happily about college life while Jason caught them up on his latest school projects. Under the cover of lively dinner chatter, Jane risked a glance at Trevor. He was listening attentively to Casey, nodding along to her story. Still an excellent listener, just as Jane remembered. He'd always made her feel both heard and seen.

She jerked her gaze away before anyone noticed her staring at him. *Get a grip! Just make it through this meal.*

"Mom makes the best étouffée." Jason patted his belly.

Jane smiled. "Why, thank you, sweetie."

Drew and Trevor both murmured agreement as

they enjoyed second helpings. At least her cooking had won over hearts.

When a lull descended, Jane racked her brain for another benign topic. She couldn't think of anything, so she fell back on dessert.

"Who wants beignets? I stopped by the bakery on the way home from work."

That did the trick. The kids cheered as she brought the fried doughnuts sprinkled with powdered sugar to the table.

Over the sugary dessert, chatter resumed again.

Jane slowly relaxed. They would get through this visit without messy reveals. She just needed to make it to Sunday when Trevor and Drew would head home, but how in the world would she keep everyone occupied tonight? If she let the kids go off on their own, she'd be stuck alone with Trevor, and that was the last thing she needed.

"Who wants to help me put up the Christmas tree?" Jane asked, injecting extra cheer into her voice.

"We'd love that, wouldn't we, honey?" Drew said, slipping his arm around Casey's waist.

Casey turned to beam at him. "Oh, yes. Our first time decorating a Christmas tree together."

Jane noticed how close they seemed. She bit her

bottom lip. If they were really serious, that meant she and Trevor—

No, Jane shut that thought down quick. No borrowing trouble. *If*, and with Casey that was a big *if*, her daughter and Drew got serious, Jane would worry about the implications then.

She glanced up and saw Trevor had noticed their kids closeness as well.

Jane put on a big smile. "Y'all kids drag the tree out of the storage shed while I wash the dishes, then we'll have a tree decorating party."

"Can we let Henry out of the basement?" Drew asked.

"Oh sure," Jane said. "Just keep a close eye on him. We want to prevent him from accidentally eating Christmas ornaments."

"Will do." Drew and Casey headed for the downstairs suite to retrieve the hound dog while Jason dug the key to the shed out of the junk drawer.

"I'll help you with the dishes," Trevor said.

"No, no, I've got this. You help the kids."

"I insist." Something in his tone of voice told her he had something to discuss with her out of earshot of their children.

"All right then."

Once the back door slammed closed after the

young people and Henry, Trevor turned to her. "I'll load the dishwasher while you wipe down the cabinets."

Well, here he was, taking charge in her kitchen as if he owned the place. Jane started to protest, but he was helpful, and she didn't want to make a mountain out of an ant hill. Even so, the room seemed to shrink with him in her space, working alongside.

It felt too... intimate.

"More wine?" he asked as he plucked the bottle from the table.

"No, thanks. I'm good."

She noticed the physical changes in Trevor. He had filled out from the tall, lanky young man he'd been in college. He was still lean, though, as if he worked out regularly but his shoulders were broader. His blond hair was still thick but a darker shade than it had been. He even smelled the same, woodsy and manly.

He'd aged well, but she wished he hadn't. Maybe then she would have laughed this off with a cool *c'est la vie* shrug if he'd lost his hair and gained a paunch. But Jane felt the ancient tug pull her closer to him, as her head protested her foolish heart.

They cleaned the kitchen with little conversation, Trevor whistling under his breath a familiar tune she couldn't quite place. Something else that hadn't changed. Trevor whistling while he worked. It was an adorable quirk really, and she was alarmed to discover she had missed it.

"What are you whistling?" she asked.

Trevor stopped whistling and looked chagrinned. "Sorry, bad habit. My whistling used to drive Laura bonkers and mostly I stopped doing it, but since she's been gone, I fell back into old habits."

"No need to apologize. It sounds cheerful. I like it."

He beamed, his eyes crinkling at the corners. "Thanks."

"Did *you* want any more of the wine?" she asked.

"Nah, I'm good." He finished loading the dishwasher, put in the soap, and closed it up.

She poured out the small amount of wine remaining in the bottle and dropped it into the glass recycle bin.

"Are you okay?" he asked.

Was she?

"Yes, of course, why wouldn't I be?"

"This situation *is* unsettling."

"I'm fine." She wanted to ask him personal questions that burned in her throat like acid that needed purging, but she refrained.

"You don't look okay."

"But I am."

"There's something we should consider."

Jane crossed her arms and leaned against the counter on the opposite side of the kitchen from him. "What's that?"

"It seems our kids are moving toward something serious—possibly even permanent. We will have to navigate that. We might even share grandchildren one day."

Jane sucked in her breath. *Have mercy!* That hadn't even occurred to her. She gulped and blinked. "I-I don't even know what to say about that."

"We shouldn't put our old baggage on them or let our old relationship mess up their new one. Agreed?"

"I would never do that to my child."

"Good, because Casey is the first girl Drew's ever asked me to meet, so this weekend is significant. I just wanted you to know that."

Oh, dear heavens, Casey might be in love for real this time. "The very first one?"

"Yes." He moved over to where she stood, his voice now softer than before. "You were the first girl I'd introduced to my parents too, remember?"

How could she ever forget? A flush swept

through her at the memory. She'd been so nervous, but his parents had welcomed her with open arms, and she'd fallen in love with the Gardners as surely as she'd fallen in love with Trevor.

Jane closed her eyes. This wouldn't be easy.

"Janie—" He touched her shoulder.

Her eyes flew open then, her sanity returning. She could never forget what he'd done. How he had abandoned her when she needed him most. She shrugged off his warm, familiar touch. She couldn't allow him to slip under her guard.

"Let's get this Christmas decorating party started, shall we?" She arched her eyebrows at him and folded her arms over her chest.

"Okay," he said. "I get it. You're still not ready to discuss the past, but when you are, I'll be waiting."

He turned to the mudroom where the kids were coming through the back door with the tree box and the ornaments.

And it was only then that Jane recognized the tune he'd been whistling. It was *their* song. Faith Hill's "This Kiss."

FIVE

Trevor helped the kids set up the artificial Christmas tree while Jane finished cleaning the kitchen.

A few minutes later, just as they were fluffing out the tree branches, Jane entered the room and put on some holiday music. Trevor couldn't help tracking her movements, his gaze zeroing in on her as the jaunty refrain of "Jingle Bell Rock" rolled out into the room.

She moved to open one of the boxes that Drew and Jason had carried in, the material of her jeans stretching across her backside, leaving no doubt that she worked out regularly and took diligent care of herself. *Stairmaster,* he guessed and felt a strange tugging in the center of his chest.

Jane straightened, caught his eye, and smiled.

Dangerous territory. Trevor dragged his gaze from her devastating grin. *Focus on literally anything else.*

"Should we get started decorating?" Jane asked.

Oh yeah. This was going to be fun. Nothing like hanging ornaments and tinsel to distract from the romantic wreckage of their past.

"Yes!" Her kids swooped in, digging in the boxes and picking their favorite ornaments from childhood. Casey and Drew exchanged stories about their past Christmases. They kept exchanging shy glances and edging closer to each other.

His son was serious about Casey, Trevor realized with a sinking feeling.

Trying his best to act normally, Trevor helped Casey and Drew untangle a strand of lights. Across the room, Jane and Jason unboxed a Christmas village for the mantel. Easy banter flowed between his son and Jane's daughter as the young couple draped

lights around the tree. Trevor envied the uncomplicated affection between them. He and Jane had once
been like that, a million years ago.

Jane leaned in to replace a fuse that had gone out
in one of the light strands. She was so close that if
Trevor moved his elbow, he'd graze her shoulder.

Her rose-scented perfume invaded his senses and
stirred memories of walks with her through the
botanical gardens at one springtime event and
suddenly the past felt more real than the present. In a
blink, they could've been those carefree college kids
again, falling in love for the first time.

No pain, no baggage.

Until there was nothing *but* pain and baggage.

"Wow! Here it is!" Jason whooped and pulled
out a Teenage Mutant Ninja Turtle ornament. "Dad
gave this to me when I was in second grade and
obsessed with the Ninja Turtles." He held the ornament for a few seconds as if absorbing its memories
before he smiled and put it on the tree.

Yeah, speaking of baggage, this box of ornaments
was filled with Jane's past from her husband David.
Just like his life was chockfull Laura memories.

"Remember this?" Casey held up a glass ornament of a waffle. "One year we decorated the tree
only in food-oriented ornaments."

"Here's the syrup ornament if you want to put it side by side with the waffle." Jane handed the bauble to Casey.

"Sounds like y'all had some pretty great Christmases." Trevor placed hooks on the ornaments and handed them to the kids to hang.

Jane's smile turned wistful. "Yes, we did. I'm so glad y'all are here to help put up the tree. I can't tell you how much I appreciate it."

"Hey, Mom," Jason said. "We're happy to do it."

"And we're creating even more memories." Casey clapped and did a little twirl.

Yes, indeed.

"It's fun." Drew beamed at Casey, and she beamed back at him.

Trevor shot a glance at Jane to see how she was gauging their kids' relationship. It looked pretty solid to Trevor.

Jane was staring off into space, a wistful expression on her beautiful face. Was she thinking about her late husband? Or maybe, dare he hope, she was thinking about the same thing he was. How close they'd been when they were young? Just as close as Drew and Casey were now.

She blinked and met his gaze.

They shared a tentative, bittersweet smile, then

both of them glanced away, but not before a simmering spark passed between them... if only for a split second.

Trevor busied himself anchoring down all the lights, trying to ignore his racing pulse. *Get a grip, man.* Whatever they'd once shared was long dead and buried in the past where it belonged.

"Anybody want cocoa?" Jane asked, sounding a little breathless.

"Me," all three young people said.

"Coming right up."

Did she need help? Or was she, like him, looking for a way out of their proximity? He didn't know, but he had to at least offer to help. "Need a hand?"

"No." The quick shake of her head brooked no argument.

Message received. Back off.

Trevor raised both palms and went over to help Drew sort through the ribbons and garlands as Bing Crosby's voice coated the room in "White Christmas."

Once Jane had escaped to the safety of the kitchen, Trevor leaned back against the couch cushion and exhaled a shaky breath. He had to lock down his emotions. Take it slow, protect himself, and not rush headlong into heartbreak again.

Because no matter how hard he tried, he couldn't deny his growing attraction to Jane.

A few minutes later, she returned with five steaming mugs on a tray, and Trevor had disappeared to the back of the tree, stringing garland. When he came around the other side, Jane was there with two mugs left on her tray.

He met her eyes. Illuminated by the glow of Christmas lights, she looked like an angel. Perfection in all her arresting glory.

Jane passed him a mug and offered him a squirt of whipped cream from the aerosol canister.

He shook his head. He'd never been a whipped cream kind of guy, but back in the day, he'd let Jane fill his cup with the foamy stuff. Now, he had stronger boundaries and didn't present as liking something that he didn't enjoy just to please someone else as he'd done when he was young.

"No, thanks," he said. "Not my jam."

"You're missing out." She winked and shot a big dollop of whipped cream to her mug, just the way she liked it.

His mind flooded with images of another Christmas where they'd shared whipped cream kisses over the mugs of cocoa in the kitchen of her parents' house. He'd enjoyed licking it right off her lips when no one was watching.

Some things a man just couldn't forget.

Jane sipped her cocoa, closing her eyes blissfully. "Mmm."

Trevor downed his cocoa and went back to stringing garland. Across the room, laughter erupted as Drew said something to make Casey snort cocoa out her nose.

Trevor peered over to see Jane suppress a grin. She was happy that her daughter was happy and that, in turn, made Trevor happy.

After he'd finished the garland, Trevor went back to helping the others hang the remaining ornaments. He went halfway up the ladder to fill in the empty spots, while Casey, Drew, and Jason loaded the lower branches.

Jane passed ornaments up to Trevor on the ladder.

"Could you please put this one near the very top?" Jane asked him. "It's the first ornament David and I ever bought together."

The knickknack was a purple and gold tragic-comedy mask of Thalia and Melpomene, not really Christmassy but very New Orleans. He wondered if David had been the artsy type. Didn't matter. Trevor wasn't.

He reached for the mask ornament and their fingers brushed.

The brief contact blistered sparks down his spine and almost knocked him off the ladder. He wrapped his free hand around the top rung to steady himself. Without thinking, he glanced down at her upturned face.

Jane met his gaze, her eyes luminous, her mouth opened slightly, teeth parted. He saw his own conflicted longing reflected in her eyes.

Trevor swayed on the ladder as the urge to kiss her hit him like a wrecking ball. *Whoa. Defcon One. Halt! Halt!*

As if sensing his rising panic, Jane gave his ankle a reassuring squeeze. If he'd been shaky before, now he was a liquid human, his heart melting into a puddle.

"It's okay," she whispered. "One step at a time."

Was she talking about his ascent up the ladder, or something else entirely? he wondered.

"You'll have to go up the last rung to reach the spot," she said. Her eyes said she'd erringly read the question on his face.

Right.

He needed to shut off his flights of fantasy before

he did something illogical... like give in to the magnetic pull between them.

Trevor hung the ornament where she guided, hyperaware of Jane's every movement below him— the way she gestured, so lithe and delicate, how her nose scrunched slightly when she stepped back to survey his handiwork and give him a thumbs-up.

They finished decorating under a cloud of melancholic nostalgia. Despite the bittersweet pang in his chest, Trevor had to admit the completed tree was a stunner, glittering proudly beneath its twinkling lights.

"It's gorgeous," Casey said. Clearly, she did not pick up on the angst fogging the air between him and Jane. Which was a relief. They were keeping things under wraps from their kids.

For now, anyway.

"Totally. We did an awesome job." Drew draped his arm around Casey's shoulder as they gazed at the tree.

Trevor climbed down the ladder.

Jane moved closer to reposition an ornament that was hanging askew, and his heart gave a strange hop.

"It just feels right, doesn't it?" Jane murmured

without looking at him. "Being together like this again."

Trevor's throat tightened. "Jane..."

She turned to him then, eyes glistening in the Christmas lights. "I know the past can't be erased with a few twinkling bulbs, but this feels like a step forward, doesn't it?"

A step toward what, he wanted to ask, but the fragile hope in her eyes made him pause. They'd loved deeply once. Could there be a path back from the ashes?

Jane gave him an encouraging smile, just the smallest crust of hope that lit up his nerve-endings.

Across the room, their kids laughed together on the couch, the picture of contentment. Trevor ached at the easy affection between Drew and Casey, so different from his and Jane's fraught history. He wished for them the very best life offered, whether it was together or apart. They both deserved a wonderful life.

He turned back to the Christmas tree, its cheerful beauty bolstering him. They'd made it through decorating the tree without a glitch. That had to count for something.

"And now," Jason said. "For the crowning glory. The star."

Jason and Drew held the ladder so Casey could climb up and place it. Jane met Trevor's gaze, mirth dancing in her eyes.

His heart stuttered. Oh, he was in trouble. Trevor glanced away to see Henry sniffing the tree base.

"Down boy!" he said a little too loud because he was warning himself as much as the hound dog.

Henry gave him I-gotta-pee eyes.

"I'm just going to take Henry out for a bit." Patting his left leg for Henry to heel at his side, Trevor escaped out the back door with his dog and most of his dignity intact.

✱✱✱✱✱✱✱✱✱✱✱✱

What an enchanting evening.

Floating on a rosy cloud of tree-decorating after-glow, Jane drifted upstairs. The guests and her kids were ensconced in their rooms, and the house was locked tight and the alarm set. It had been so nice having help with decorating and entertaining the kids. Until Trevor, she hadn't realized how much the holidays had overwhelmed her after David's passing.

Tonight had been so easy. Not at all what she'd expected when she first realized that Trevor was Drew's dad.

As she readied for bed, she took her phone from her pocket and saw she'd gotten a text from Suzy. It was simple and to the point.

> ???

> It went fine.

> Fine? What do you mean fine?

> It was a nice evening.

> Nice as in...?

> We ate dinner, put up & decorated the tree, drank cocoa, & listened to Christmas music.

> And?

And she and Trevor had shared a look over the growing closeness of their adult children, but she didn't feel like sharing that with Suzy. Not yet. She knew her friend would warn her off rekindling anything with Trevor and it was sound advice. She just didn't want to hear it right now.

> There's no 'and.'

How were things with Trevor?

Nice.

Uh-oh.

No uh-oh. Don't do that. I'm glad things are nice since Casey and Drew seem serious. It'll make life easier if Trevor and I have an amiable relationship.

Yeah, okay, sure. Keep telling yourself that.

What are you suggesting?

If you're not careful, he's going to hurt you all over again.

No worries. I have my head screwed on tight.

Good, 'cause you know what they say...

What's that?

Once a runner, always a runner.

SIX

At dawn, Trevor went running with Henry, slipping out of the house while everyone else slept in. Thank heavens Jane had shown him how to disarm the alarm last night before they'd all gone to bed so he could leave without waking the household.

He couldn't stop thinking about the previous evening and how much fun he'd had with Jane and their kids.

Henry loped along beside him as Trevor trotted through Jane's quaint neighborhood. She'd done well in life, and he was impressed with all she'd achieved. One thing was clear, she hadn't needed him.

Not in the least.

He and Jane had a passionate and exciting relationship in another life. Young and in love, with so many plans for a future together. They'd been head over heels. It had all been so thrilling.

When things ended, it had blown Trevor's world apart. The actual breakup was fuzzy after all these years, altered by time and memory. Oh, not the events that led to their breakup, but the emotions and reasons why they'd both reacted the way they had.

Would they ever have an opportunity to talk it through? Or was the past still too difficult for Jane to discuss? He'd been in the wrong, so for forgiveness, the ball was in her court.

Despite the despair that had eaten him up after losing Jane, Trevor had met a grounded, down-to-earth woman in Laura. They'd been blessed with twenty-two years of happiness together. Their love grew slowly over time and was born from friendship, common interests, and shared strong family values.

Maybe they'd never been as hot for each other as he and Jane had been, but Laura had been his helpmate.

He was incredibly proud of their son and the life he and Laura had built together. To say he'd made a terrible mistake leaving Jane felt like negating the life he'd led. No, things had happened the way they were supposed to.

And now?

With Jane?

Well, if his feelings last night were any sign, he was just as attracted to her as he'd ever been, and she seemed magnetized by him too.

Trevor *had* made a fatal error with Jane, and he wasn't proud of it. Seeing her again reminded him of things he'd forgotten. An old yearning had taken hold last night when their fingers had brushed while decorating the tree. A hot spark. A trail of longing looks. Smiles that held both memories and promises.

That kind of love didn't come around twice in a lifetime. "*Crazy love*" was what his dad had called it back then. Saying that now was considered ableist, but his dad had been right.

Trevor and Jane *had* loved each other to the point of madness.

No matter how much he might want to rekindle something with Jane, he needed to keep that in mind. He wouldn't lose his head again. He was older, wiser, and understood how real, lasting love worked. Besides, he wouldn't do anything that might cause problems for Drew and Casey. He and Jane might have gotten it wrong, but their children sure deserved to get it right.

On quiet feet, he jogged up Jane's driveway, slowed to a walk, and let himself in through the back door.

Just as Jane came down the stairs.

Not in a bathrobe and slippers as Laura would have been, but fully dressed, hair styled and makeup on—elegant as always.

"Hey," he said, feeling exposed in his running shorts and T-shirt. "How'd you sleep?"

"Wonderfully. You?"

"Okay." He hedged because he'd tossed and turned all night, plagued by the memory of their hands touching, and he wasn't about to say that.

Henry's tail thumped against the mudroom wall, and he looked up at Jane with delight in his eyes.

I know how you feel, old fella.

"Good morning to you too, Henry." Jane crouched in front of the hound dog, made cooing noises, and scratched him behind the ears.

Henry's tail went wild, and it matched the

rhythm of Trevor's rapidly beating heart. Looking at Jane, bent over Henry, gave him an unobstructed view down her blouse. Unsettled by his body's response, Trevor jerked his gaze away just as Jane rose to her feet.

"Kids still asleep?" he asked.

"I haven't heard a peep, so I'm assuming yes."

"I'm glad they're all getting along so well."

"Drew is an amazing young man. You've done an excellent job raising him, Trevor. I know it hasn't been easy for you after losing your wife."

"Thanks. And Casey seems to bring out the best in him."

"The kids want to go to Brennan's tonight for dinner if we can get a reservation. It's been their favorite spot since they were little."

"I'll handle the reservation on my restaurant app." He held up his cell phone and pulled up the app. He leafed through the availabilities on the website. "Nothing at Brennan's until nine."

"Nine's a bit late for me these days. See what Pascal's has."

Pascal's.

A fresh batch of memories filled Trevor's mind. The two of them sitting side by side at a table in Pascal's, feeding each other bites of barbecue shrimp to celebrate him getting his undergraduate degree.

She made a soft noise, and he glanced up to see a vague look in her eyes as if she too was remembering the restaurant and the memories they'd made there.

"We could go somewhere else," he said.

"No, no." She shook her head. "Pascal's is fine."

He nodded and tapped his phone screen. "They've got a table for five at seven. Should I grab it?"

"Yes, let's do that and make it a party of six. Suzy is joining us at Casey's request."

"Suzy, huh? How is she?"

"She's great. We're in business together."

"No kidding? What kind of business?"

Jane told him about their design firm that specialized in historic renovation. "I do the renovation planning, and she specializes in décor."

"I can't wait to hear more about it." He stood there looking at her. She was so close. Close enough to kiss. "Well, I'm pretty sweaty. I'm gonna go shower. Do you mind if I leave Henry here with you?"

"Not at all. In the meantime, I'll start breakfast."

"If you can wait ten minutes, I'll give you a hand," he offered.

"No, thanks," she said, shutting down his hopes. "I've got it all together."

Then she turned and went into the kitchen and all Trevor could think as he watched her walk away was *oh yes, you do*.

✦✦✦✦✦✦✦✦✦✦✦✦

Jane was just about to start breakfast when the three young people converged on the kitchen. They announce they wanted to take Jane and Trevor out for beignets and coffee at the café down the street. Jane wasn't particularly spontaneous, and it took her a minute to readjust when the plans suddenly changed.

"How about we walk down St. Charles with Henry?" Casey suggested.

"Let's take Mom's SUV," Jason said. "That's over a mile away."

"Lazy." Casey stuck out her tongue at her brother.

"Walking is a great idea," Jane said, intervening. "It'll only take twenty minutes or so, and it's a nice morning."

"I guess I can do it for beignets." Jason feigned reluctance. Her son was a beignet fiend and would do anything for the sugar-dusted fried dough.

The five of them started out for the coffee shop, walking abreast down the driveway, but the narrow sidewalk forced them into smaller groups. The young adults wandered ahead, leaving Jane and Trevor with Henry on his leash to bring up the rear.

In college, she and Trevor used to walk from the campus to a franchise of the same outdoor café for a beignet run every Sunday morning. She wondered if he remembered that.

As they walked, Jane suppressed a yawn.

"Do you lie about sleeping wonderfully?" Trevor asked.

"Maybe." She shrugged and gave him a sheepish grin. "A little. I don't sleep well many nights, so if I sleep better than that, to me it's wonderful."

"I know what that's like," he said.

"Since David passed away..." She inhaled sharply. "No, you don't want to hear about my late husband. Oh, look at the Christmas decorations on the Millers' house. I wonder where they found an inflatable Grinch that immense?"

Trevor touched her elbow.

She froze in her tracks, bringing Trevor to a stop

as well. Jane stared down at his hand as instant heat blasted from his fingertips into her skin.

Quickly, he dropped his arm and his gaze. "I apologize. That was out of line. I shouldn't have touched you."

"It's all right." She rested the right elbow he'd touched in her left palm.

"I just wanted to tell you it's okay if you want to talk about David." His eyes met hers. "I'm happy to listen."

"Really?"

"Really."

"Hey, you slowpokes." hands cupped around her mouth, Casey called from halfway down the block with Jason and Drew. "Hurry up!"

Jane, who didn't want to holler in the quiet neighborhood on a Saturday morning, motioned for them to go on ahead.

"You were saying?" Trevor prompted when they started walking again.

It was kind of him to listen to her. "Since David had passed away, being alone in the house at night is unsettling."

"Too quiet," Trevor said.

"Yes."

"I get it."

They shared a glance. He really did understand, and she felt a vine of connection twine between them.

"Seems we've found ourselves at a similar place in life. We've been thrown curveballs, the both of us," she said.

"Yeah. Losing Laura pulled the rug out from under my feet."

"Losing a spouse changes everything."

He nodded. "Such a big loss disrupts plans and makes you realize that each day truly is precious."

"Precious," she echoed.

"No time left to waste."

Their gazes welded and Jane felt her pulse quicken.

"Listen, Jane, I hope we can be friends for the kids' sake. What happened between us is in the past. Can we let go of it? What do you say?"

"I can do friendly," she said. "Not sure I'm ready to be friends with you, Trevor. That's a big ask. How about we take our leads from the kids? We'll cross that bridge if and when Casey and Drew deepen their relationship."

"I guess that's a start, huh?"

She nodded and as they kept walking, she widened the distance between them.

They arrived at the coffee shop and ordered café au lait and several orders of beignets. Since beignets always came in orders of three, they placed four orders.

It was early enough that they could sit at a couple of outdoor tables and enjoy the coolness of the morning as they watched humanity stroll by. There were a couple of water bowls and some treats for Henry outside the restaurant door. New Orleans was a pet-friendly place these days.

Drew sucked in powdered sugar on his first bite and went into a small coughing fit. "Don't inhale when you take a bite." Casey laughed and slapped him on the back.

"My bad. Mmm. These are awesome."

Jane recalled her and Trevor's Sunday morning trips to their coffee shop again. She shot a glance at him to see if he was thinking the same thing.

A slight smile edged the corner of his mouth.

Four years of Sunday mornings with coffee and beignets. Back then, those four years seemed like an eternity. Four years had shaped her as a young woman. A woman who'd thought she'd found a soulmate and trusted that she and Trevor would last a lifetime.

"Hey, Mom, did you get a dinner reservation at

Brennan's?" Jason asked. His brain usually moved to the next meal while eating the current one.

"Brennan's was booked up until nine. But we got in at Pascal's. How does that sound?"

"Best barbecue shrimp in the city. That works." Jason grinned, a ring of powdered sugar around his lips.

"Once we finish here, how about a stroll through the park?" Trevor asked. "Work off the beignet calories."

Everyone was up for the idea. After breakfast, they walked through the park for half an hour amidst the old moss-strung oaks and duck ponds, with Casey pointing out some of her favorite spots to Drew. Henry got excited when he caught sight of the ducks, and Trevor had to tighten up on his leash.

"Look, Mom!" Casey pointed beyond the treetops. "A Ferris wheel. There must a carnival nearby."

Drew checked a phone app. "Yeah, there's a Christmas carnival a few blocks away set up in an area usually reserved for flea markets."

"Can we go?" Casey asked, her eyes lively.

Jane shot Trevor a look.

He shrugged. "Why not?"

"We can't go on the Ferris wheel with the dog," Jane pointed out.

"No worries," Drew said. "We can all take turns riding while someone stays with Henry."

"My boy's a problem solver." Trevor grinned.

Even at eleven o'clock in the morning, the carnival was already a hubbub of activity. Holding hands, Casey and Drew made a beeline for the Ferris wheel.

"Those two have it bad for each other," Jason said.

Jane and Trevor exchanged glances, then watched as Casey and Drew went to the ticket booth and bought tickets.

Jason trailed after Casey and Drew to the Ferris wheel queue. A few minutes later, the three of them climbed onto the Ferris wheel. Casey and Drew sitting together in a car, Jason riding solo.

Jane and Trevor waited as Henry eagerly sniffed the ground, exploring the environment. Immediately to their left was a small roller coaster built to look like an elaborate mousetrap. Passengers screamed as the cars soared, then plummeted. To the right were bumper cars, and straight ahead lay the merry-go-round. From the nearby arcade, carnival barkers called, urging people to try their luck at Christmas-themed games of chance. There was Santa ring toss, blow-up reindeer balloon with a water gun, and Whack-an-Elf.

"Remember when you won me that giant stuffed panda at a carnival just like this one?" Jane said.

"It cost me eighty bucks to win the dang thing," Trevor said, "but I refused to stop until I did."

The sweet memory washed over her. "I loved that panda so much, even as it came unsewn at the seams a few weeks later because I hugged it so much."

They smiled at each other.

"We did have some good times, didn't we?"

"That we did," Jane murmured. *Until it all went awry.*

After their ride on the Ferris wheel, the kids came over, chattering about the view from the top. "You can see Jackson Square," Casey said.

"How do you know?" Jason said. "You guys were smooching up a storm."

"Hey." Casey playfully punched her brother in the upper arm. "Mind your own business."

"Here, Dad," Drew said, ducking his head to hide a blush, and held out his hand to Trevor. "Give me Henry's leash so you and Jane can have a turn."

Jane held up her palms. "That's okay. I've been on enough Ferris wheels in my life."

"No," Casey said, taking Jane's arms and

propelling her toward the Ferris wheel. "It's time for you to have some fun, Mom."

Drew nudged his dad along to the Ferris wheel as well.

"The more we resist, the more they'll persist, it seems," Trevor said to Jane. "Might as well surrender."

"Okay, fine. One turn on the Ferris wheel, but I am *not* going on the roller coaster."

"Deal," Casey said, handing the ticket taker two tickets for Jane and Trevor.

The next thing Jane knew, she and Trevor were sitting side by side in the Ferris wheel car. Their kids were on the ground waving at them as their cage cycled upward and the noises from the carnival lessened the higher they rose. She was achingly aware of Trevor's nearness and to calm her nerves, she clutched the grab bar with both hands.

At the top, Jane spied Jackson Square. "Do you remember our first Mardi Gras together?"

"How could I forget? We ended up in Jackson Square having our fortunes told by a very scary-looking palm reader," Trevor said. "Madam Leveaux said we were fated."

"So much for that, huh?" Jane snorted an indelicate laugh.

"If I recall, she did say we'd have rocky times before we got to our happily ever after."

Jane sucked in a deep breath and turned to look at him. "I don't remember that part."

"I remember because it troubled me."

"Really?"

He nodded.

They sat in silence as the Ferris wheel rolled downward and Jackson Square disappeared from their view, wiping out the past.

Then Trevor, lightly and so briefly, reached over and brushed his thumb across her knuckles.

Instead of pulling back as her common sense urged, Jane turned her palm up and interlaced their fingers.

And they held hands until the car they were riding in reached the ground.

SEVEN

Trevor couldn't stop thinking about their Ferris wheel ride as he dressed for dinner. When Jane turned her palm up and interlaced their fingers, he'd been stunned, but eager to hold her hand.

Now he felt dazed and a bit dazzled with possibility.

"What do you think, boy?" he asked Henry. "Maybe Jane and I could..."

Could what? He needed to shut down that line of thinking. This weekend was about Drew and Casey, not Trevor and Jane.

Henry studied him with a noncommittal expression.

"You're right. I need to push these thoughts out of my mind."

Rubbing the palm that had interlaced with Jane's, Trevor smiled and slipped into his sports jacket. The restaurant was only a few blocks from Jane's house, and they'd discussed walking instead of taking a vehicle. It was cool outside, but not cold enough for a coat. A light jacket would suffice.

Tomorrow was Sunday, and he was wistful about returning home, wishing he could spend more time with Jane and the kids. And he was determined to mend fences with Jane, which meant they should dig into their past at some point.

Not a chore he looked forward to, but what had happened between them had left a scar on his psyche... and his heart. He needed her forgiveness. Purging the hurt and anger and moving forward would do them both good.

Well, it would do him good, anyway. He hoped it would do the same for her.

He refilled Henry's water bowl and threw him a

chew toy. Just as he was about to go upstairs, a knocked sounded at his bedroom door.

"Dad?" Drew opened the door and stuck his head into the room.

"Hi, kiddo. I was just on my way upstairs."

"Can I talk to you for a second before you do?"

"Sure, sure." Trevor waved him into the room.

Drew stepped inside and closed the door behind him. His son looked happy. More than happy. He was practically vibrating with joy.

"What do you think about Casey?" Drew asked.

A little surprised, Trevor said, "I think she's lovely, son."

"She's the one, Dad. You always told me I would know it when I met the right girl, and you were right, as usual."

He stared at his boy, who was now a man. The one who loved to fish, excelled in school, and was respectful to people without being a pushover. Trevor was so proud of him.

"I'm happy for you, Drew. Your mother would have loved Casey."

"Thanks, Dad." They clapped each other on the back and Trevor blinked away the mistiness in his eyes.

He was thrilled for his son, but Drew's

announcement put Trevor's focus back on his relationship with Jane. The likelihood they could become in-laws was real now. He needed to speak to Jane and considering the circumstances, the sooner the better.

✶✶✶*✶✶✶✶*✶✶*✶*

Jane had one goal for the evening. Get through it without Suzy rocking the boat. While she loved her friend dearly, Suzy spoke her mind freely. Jane admired her friend's forthrightness, but sometimes Suzy could be bristly. Especially if she perceived an injustice.

And in Suzy's mind, Trevor had done Jane wrong. Never mind that it had been twenty-five years ago. Suzy had a long memory.

The five of them strolled toward the restaurant, carefully navigating the sidewalks where the tree roots had lifted the concrete or broken through, causing large cracks here and there. It was the same all over the city because there were so many old trees near the streets. It made for a shady but bumpy walk.

Jane wore a red jersey wrap dress that hit her just above her knees, paired with low-heeled red pumps. High heels were no longer an option since they caused horrible foot cramps. When she'd been younger, she hadn't thought twice about sporting four or five-inch heels every day. She missed the high heels, but getting older did have its advantages, like no longer caring what other people thought of her footwear.

"You look fantastic." Trevor's eyebrows lifted.

"Thanks." Her first instinct was to tell him he also looked handsome—which he did—in his turtleneck, sport coat, and dark jeans, but saying so felt too intimate.

"Where's Suzy?" Trevor asked Jane as they again lagged after the young adults. "Didn't you say she was joining us for dinner?"

"She's meeting us at the restaurant."

"Does she know I'm here?"

"She does."

"What did she say?"

"Her text had several emojis, so I doubt you'd want to know." She cocked a brow at him and grinned.

"Suzy was always my biggest fan," he said. "Until she wasn't."

"Yes, well, she's my oldest and most loyal friend. You should have expected her to take my side."

"Jane," he said. "About that—"

But Jane wasn't ready to talk about the past. Particularly when the kids were around. She still felt weird from that moment on the Ferris wheel, afraid that Trevor had already started reading something into it. She'd been feeling nostalgic and held his hand for a few minutes. So what? It meant nothing.

She scooted ahead of him, hurrying to catch up with the kids as they opened the door and stepped into Pascal's.

Jane gave the hostess their name, and a server led them to a table where Suzy was already waiting with a glass of wine in front of her and an open bottle on the table.

Suzy's gaze grabbed Jane's, and they exchanged a look. A look between friends who'd shared pretty much everything that life had thrown their way since childhood.

Are you okay? Suzy mouthed silently.

Jane nodded and watched Suzy shift her attention to Trevor, narrow her eyes, and frown at him.

Casey and Jason hugged Suzy, and Casey introduced her godmother to Drew. Suzy shook Drew's hand and engaged him in casual chitchat.

Jane had texted Suzie and reminded her not to give away to the kids that she knew Trevor. Suzy had half-heartedly agreed, asking Jane why she didn't just tell the kids the truth. But why go through all that if Casey and Drew didn't have staying power? No, it was much more civilized to keep their personal business under wraps.

At least for now.

"Suzy, this is Trevor, Drew's father. Trevor, this is my oldest friend, Suzy."

Suzy squinted hard and shook his hand. Suzy had a powerful handshake and Jane knew she was squeezing his hand hard. "Nice to *meet* you, Trevor."

"You too." His tone was neutral, revealing nothing.

Yay. They were both going to keep the past buried. She smiled at Suzy and then at Trevor, thanking them for their silence.

Jane sat next to Suzy and Trevor settled in beside Jane. The young adults carried the conversation. The barbeque shrimp and garlic bread were delicious, as always, and the kids' laughter was infectious.

She tried her best to relax and enjoy the food. But it was nerve-racking with Suzy and Trevor eyeing each other like mortal enemies forced into an unwanted detente.

If Suzy let something slip about Jane and Trevor's past, it would cast them both in a negative light. Jane rarely omitted things from her children, so this would seem like an outright lie should they get caught. A tangled web indeed.

Maybe you should just tell them now.

Jane considered it, then nixed the idea. Everyone was having so much fun, and the kids all looked so happy. Plus, she really didn't want to get into the gory details of her past with Trevor. And if Drew and Casey weren't serious about each other, really there was no point.

"Mr. Gardner," Casey said, taking her attention off Drew for half a second. "Mom and Suzy are in business together and they're renovating that Harlow house in the Garden District on St. Charles. It's a big deal."

"Really?" Drew said. "That's impressive, Mrs. L."

Hmm, when had Drew decided to get informal and call her Mrs. L instead of by her last name? Jane couldn't decide whether she liked it or not.

"John Harlow's home?" Trevor asked.

In college, Jane and Trevor had been close friends of John's. His family owned the house steeped in New Orleans history. During summer breaks, John lived in his parents' pool house and spent a lot of time with Trevor and Jane, swimming and sunbathing by the pool.

More memories drifted in. She and Trevor, lying side by side on matching loungers, smelling of coconut oil and soaking up the sun, holding hands until they got too sweaty. It was a simple memory that packed a big punch.

Jane peeked at Trevor. He had a pleasant smile on his face, and he seemed relaxed.

"I imagine that renovating in historic New Orleans presents some unique challenges," Trevor said.

Jane nodded. "Yes, we've just applied for all the permits from the city and the historic renovation society last week. It will be a huge job."

"But we'll have a blast, like always," Suzy said.

"I'm assuming you'll start after the holidays?" Trevor arched his eyebrows.

"Actually, no, we're start the planning on Monday," Suzy said in a sharp tone and gave Trevor a vexed scowl.

Jane imagined Suzy would have much to say about this situation once they could speak privately.

Suzy had been there to pick up the pieces for Jane after their breakup. She'd often given colorful accounts of what she'd like to do to Trevor for hurting her friend the way he had. Suzy had also been close to Jane's husband, David, so her friend was struggling to be polite throughout dinner.

Jane had never compared David to Trevor since they'd been such different men. David had been warm and loving, but quiet. Trevor had an effervescent spark that was undeniable. Still did. A comparison wasn't fair to David because her late husband had many wonderful, but less obvious qualities.

"Does the Harlow family still own the house?" Trevor asked. "I lost contact with John after college."

"Do you have trouble hanging on to friends, Mr. Gardner?" Suzy asked.

Trevor locked gazes with Suzy and gave her a mild smile. "Not at all, Ms. Guidry. People come and go in our lives. Nothing unnatural about that."

"Hmph," Suzy muttered.

Jane bumped her friend's ankle under the table and gave her a quelling look. "John's been living in France. The house sat empty for years after his parents passed away, but John is moving back home and wants to restore it to its former glory. The house is a true gem in the district—or it was. The city seems eager to get the project underway, so we're hoping they'll expedite the building permits."

"It's been a tremendous eyesore all these years—so overgrown and deserted. I imagine everyone in the area will be thrilled that it's being rebuilt," Casey told Drew.

"I think it's so cool your mom and Suzy bring historic old places back to life." Drew stared into Casey's eyes.

Casey giggled and leaned in to brush a quick kiss on his lips.

Jane had never seen her daughter kiss a boy in front of her. The fact Casey felt emboldened to do so now gave her pause. *Hmmm.*

"Are you coming home to live when you graduate, Casey?" Suzy asked, changing the topic.

Casey's smile didn't waver. "I'm not sure yet."

"And when do you graduate?" Suzy asked Drew.

"In the spring, same as Casey. Then I have an engineering internship after graduation. It'll help me in the job market."

"Smart." Suzy nodded and winked at Casey.

Well, at least her friend seemed to approve of Drew.

Their main dish arrived, and conversation drifted to college football and Jane relaxed a little. Suzy seemed less antagonist, and the kids were having a wonderful time. Before dessert arrived, Suzy pushed back from the table.

"Jane, care to accompany me to the powder room?" Suzy asked.

Uh-oh. "Sure."

Jane stood, left her linen napkin in her seat, and followed her friend to the restroom. "We'll be right back."

The bathroom door had no more closed shut than Suzy whirled around to Jane. "Those two kids are serious about each other. It's time you and Trevor sorted yourselves out and told them the truth."

"How do you know that?"

"I've known Casey her entire life and I've never seen her look at a boy the way she looks at Drew."

With a sinking feeling, Jane agreed. "I'll have a talk with her."

But even as she said it, Jane remembered her phone call with Casey when she'd told Jane she believed Drew was The One. Jane had thought it was Casey's usual exuberance for a new romance, but now that she'd met Drew and seen him with her daughter, she had to face the truth.

Her daughter was in love and Drew loved her right back.

"Right now, Trevor is the one you should be

talking to because I was watching him closely, and he kept sneaking glances at *you*."

"Me?" Jane pressed a hand to her chest.

"Oh yeah. I think the embers still burn. At least from his side."

Her side too, Jane realized with a start. She was the one who'd held hands with him, and it had felt even nicer than she recalled.

"Well?" Suzy asked, taking a lipstick from her clutch purse and leaning over the sink for a better look in the mirror as she reapplied it.

"Well, what?"

"How do you feel about Trevor?"

"Suzy, I don't even know the man anymore. Sure, we were mad for each other once upon a time, but that was long ago. We're different people now."

"And both widowed."

"What are you suggesting?"

"Life's short." Suzy shrugged. "That's all I'm saying."

"You're pushing for Trevor?" Stunned, Jane stared at her best friend.

"No. I'm pushing for your happiness and if Trevor makes you happy again... well, I can make peace with that."

"You're jumping to a lot of conclusions tonight."

"Maybe. Perhaps it's the nostalgia of seeing you and Trevor together that's got me believing the world can be redeemed." Suzy capped her lipstick and turned back to Jane.

"Really?" Hope gave Jane's heart wings.

"Maybe it's because we save old houses and I'm just feeling sentimental about the past. I'm just saying, you've been in a fog since David died and maybe it's time to reenter the land of the living."

"But with Trevor of all people?"

"Not saying you'll end up with Trevor. Just saying that you shouldn't close yourself off to opportunity when it comes strolling back into your life and looking like a million bucks."

EIGHT

On the walk back home, Jane couldn't stop thinking about what Suzy had said. She couldn't believe her friend had such a change of heart about Trevor. A man she'd once described with every curse word in her colorful vocabulary.

And as for her ex, was he really interested in rekindling their relationship as Suzy seemed to think?

Better question. Was she?

Jane snuck a glance at Trevor, who was walking beside her in the cool night air. His handsome profile was silhouetted in the glow of the Christmas lights lining the houses along Napoleon Avenue.

What was he thinking?

It had been such a nice evening that Jane didn't want it to end. Had he experienced the night in the same way she had?

Up ahead of them, Casey and Drew strolled arm in arm, while Jason trailed behind, hands shoved in his pockets, shoulders hunched against the cool breeze. Young love, so carefree. Jane envied their innocence. If only she and Trevor could recapture that simplicity.

But no, too much stood between them now. Water under the bridge, spilled milk, missed opportunities, all the cliches.

Or were they?

Suzy seemed convinced Trevor still carried at least a small torch for her. And try as she might, Jane couldn't deny her own stirring feeling. His touch on the Ferris wheel had positively singed her.

Jane sighed loudly enough to make Trevor glance over. His eyes held a question. What path did she want to take? Amiable truce, friendship, or something more perilous? Her pragmatic side warned her to be cautious with her heart.

But another part whispered she owed it to herself to discover if what they'd once shared still simmered below the surface.

As the kids disappeared into the house, Jane touched Trevor's arm. "Could we talk?"

His face softened to a gentle smile. "I'd like that."

They settled onto the porch swing, the night wrapping around them, increasing the intimacy. It was time for truth, no matter the cost. Jane steeled her nerves and turned to him, but before she could speak, he beat her to the punch.

"I think you should know Drew told me that Casey is 'the one.'"

Jane sucked in her breath. She'd suspected as much, but hearing Trevor say the words made it really real. Casey and Drew were falling head over heels and things were progressing quickly between her daughter and her former fiancé's son. It startled her to realize her daughter was a woman in love.

"Are you okay?" he asked, his tone solicitous.

"Yes. Casey told me the same thing when she asked if she could bring Drew home to meet me, but I was taking a wait and see approach. I had no idea they were really this far along."

She worried for her daughter. The risk a woman took when giving a man her heart was big. The biggest. She could only hope Casey didn't come away shattered like Jane had.

Don't make this about you and your worries. Keep the focus on Casey and Drew.

So far, the kids hadn't caught on to anything going on between their parents, for which Jane was thankful, but right now, she had to confront things with Trevor head-on.

"Trevor," Jane began, her heart hammering. "Our children's happiness must come first."

"I agree."

"Seeing you again brought up a lot of old feelings. Feelings I thought I'd tucked away years ago."

He studied her face, blue eyes gentle. "I know. It's the same for me."

Really? Hopeful goosebumps spread up her arm. But no. This wasn't the time or place for indulging her own desires.

A charged silence fell between them. So much needing saying, but it seemed neither of them knew where to start.

Finally, Trevor spoke. "I know I hurt you when I left. I deeply regret how things ended with us."

Jane wrapped her arms around herself, clasping

her elbows in opposite palms, warding off her fears as much as the chill. "Me too."

"It was a fraught time."

"The worst." She nodded.

"Do you want to dig into this now? Here?"

Jane didn't want to, but it was getting harder and harder to distinguish the past Trevor from the man sitting beside of her now. Maybe it was time.

"Why don't you start?" She gave him a faint smile.

He took a deep breath, as if searching for the courage to speak. She inhaled too, breathing in the scent of his cologne mingled with the pine-scented air.

"First of all, I am truly sorry for hurting you. I was young and stupid, and I made a selfish decision I can't take back."

That he could admit his faults was huge in her book. She nodded, listening.

"My behavior was reprehensible and even now, I can't expect you to forgive me for it, but I hope, for our kids, we can move past it."

"Of course I can forgive you. It was a quarter of a century ago. We were young. I was overly reactive. I know you didn't mean to hurt me..." She paused, then came out with her truth. "But you did."

"And it kills my soul to this day."

He looked so contrite she wanted to cup his cheek with her palm and tell him everything would be all right. She still carried the stain of that pain buried deep within her heart.

Even after twenty-five years.

He'd hurt her that much. But she was so grateful for the opportunity to make things right, get closure, and move forward. They could easily become in-laws and for the sake of their future, they needed to move past this. She was willing and clearly Trevor was, too.

"It's okay. We both had wonderful marriages and happy lives. Nothing to regret."

"But I do. I made a rash decision without considering you, and it ruined us," he said.

"You weren't completely at fault. I was pretty intractable."

"With good reason," he said. "You did nothing wrong. I take full responsibility."

"I should have tried to work things out with you instead of nursing my pain and closing myself off."

"No. You survived the best way you knew how."

"We were collateral damage of my grief over Chad."

Trevor nodded. "I know, and that's my deepest sorrow. Not understanding how serious things had become with your brother. I should have come home. I should have been there for you. I wasn't and I will live with that betrayal the rest of my life."

Jane had replayed the scenario in her head so many times over the years. Trevor had just asked her to marry him at Christmas Beach, and she'd said yes.

It had been the most thrilling moment of her life, and then he'd dropped the bombshell. He was leaving for Europe to do an internship in global medicine for six months and he'd wanted to nail down their commitment before he left.

She'd been shocked. Stunned. She'd had no clue he was planning such a trip. He told her the opportunity had just opened up, and he'd had to decide on the spot. There were hundreds of candidates, and he'd been chosen for one of only three slots. He had to let them know immediately, so he'd just said yes without running it by her first.

And then to spring it on her right after he'd asked her to marry him. Well, she'd reacted selfishly. She'd called him inconsiderate. Considering everything she and her family were going through with her brother Chad's cancer diagnosis.

And then he'd left for Europe the very next day... after she'd given him his ring back and told him it

was over. They'd both been headstrong and stub-
born, and they'd hurt each other because of it.

"Six months wasn't really that long," she said.
"But to a twenty-five-year-old, it felt like a
lifetime."

"I should have chosen an internship closer to
home. Europe dazzled me," he said. "I thought going
abroad would give me a worldview inaccessible to me
here in the states. I thought it was my only chance to
see the world."

She remembered him trying to convince her that
the international opportunity was the best thing.
Her reasoning? He hadn't even started medical
school yet, so really, why had it mattered? It wasn't as
if he got college credits for going.

"Where I really messed up was not taking Chad's
condition into full consideration. I'm sorry for that."
His voice deepened, filled with the heavy emotions of
the past. "So very sorry. I hurt you badly. You didn't
deserve that treatment."

Jane hardly allowed herself to think about losing
her precious older brother, because it was still so
painful whenever she thought about Chad. The first
great loss cut the deepest. She'd never experienced
grief like that before, and in her youth, she didn't
understand that death was a part of life. Chad had

been taken away far too soon, and she'd blamed the world.

Blamed Trevor most of all.

"There's nothing you could have done if you'd been here," she admitted.

"No, but I should have been there to support you. I could have comforted you. Instead, I was thousands of miles away." He gently touched her knee, consolation in retrospect. "You needed me, and I wasn't there."

She didn't move away from his sympathy as she would have earlier. Instead, she enjoyed the comforting weight of his palm on her knee. Steadying her.

"You couldn't know Chad would die. When you left, his chemotherapy was working. He was tolerating it well," she said, letting him off the hook in this moment as she'd been unable to do twenty-five years ago. "The odds were in his favor. What happened to him was a tragedy no one could have predicted. I see it clearly now. I couldn't see that back then."

A member of the hospital staff gave Chad the wrong chemo drug, and he had a severe reaction that caused cardiac arrest. They tried their best to save him, but her older brother had lost his life.

Then there had been a legal morass for her parents to navigate in and a sizeable settlement, but nothing could make up for losing her precious brother.

"I should have come home when it happened. But by the time news reached me in the secluded village in Italy where I was working, Chad was already buried, and you wouldn't return my calls."

"I was in too much emotional pain. I suffered such deep clinical depression. My folks even sent me to a treatment facility in California. That's where I was when you returned. That's why my folks told you I wouldn't see you. They were trying to protect me."

"I didn't know that happened," he whispered, his eyes mournful. "All I knew was that you refused to see me when I came home. I thought... well, it doesn't matter what I thought. I took the wrong path, and I regretted it. Most of all, I regret the pain and suffering that I added to your grief. I'm sorry, Jane. Truly."

He gave her knee a gentle squeeze and in that reassuring gesture she felt the depth of his remorse. Now that the words were out, and her resentment expressed and dealt with, she felt a sense of quiet peace she hadn't expected.

"Of course," he said. "I expect nothing from you now. I'm just grateful we've had this chance to reconnect and clear the air. I'm happy we can get over this for the sake of our kids."

Jane nodded, a myriad of emotions swirling through her. She wasn't ready to leap into anything, but having Trevor back in her life filled a space she hadn't realized was empty. Time would reveal what shape their renewed connection would take. For now, the next step was unclear.

"Should we head inside?" Trevor asked. "I bet the kids are wondering where we disappeared to."

Jane managed a small smile. "Probably a good idea."

"Just to let you know, I'll be leaving around noon tomorrow," he said. "I'm on call tomorrow night and need to be close to the hospital."

"I understand," she said, both sad and relieved that their time together was drawing to a close.

"This weekend has been special to me," he said. "And if nothing else, we did get some closure."

"Closure," she echoed, feeling uncertain. What she'd secretly wanted was a new beginning, but for now, closure was better than nothing.

❋❋❋❋❋❋❋❋❋❋❋❋

The next morning, Jane made waffles and bacon. Trevor and the young adults pitched in, and it was a lively breakfast filled with conversation, laughter, and enjoying each other's company.

After the dishes were done, they went to church services, Jane and Trevor sitting apart, with Casey and Drew between them while Jason sat on Jane's other side. When it came time to sing hymns, Trevor's baritone voice rang out from the other voices. She'd forgotten what a gifted singer he was. Back at Jane's house, Trevor went to the guest suite to pack up his things and collect Henry.

It was twelve thirty by the time Trevor came upstairs with his hound dog in tow. He'd been here less than less than forty-eight hours and yet so much had changed in that brief time. She was going to miss having him in the house, and that surprised her.

He cut a handsome figure in jeans and a western shirt, cowboy boots, and Stetson. Jane's heart pitter-patted.

"Well, I guess that's it," he said. "Thanks again

for letting me stay here. This weekend has been a lot of fun."

"I enjoyed it."

"Me too."

She smiled. He smiled back. His gaze lingered on hers.

"We accomplished something," he said.

"Yes. We did."

Jane followed Trevor and Henry out to his truck. "So, will I see you sometime during the holidays?"

"If not, I guess it'll be at graduation in Ruston this spring. Jane, I—" The longing in his eyes made Jane believe he was about to say something important, but Drew came out of the house and hurried over. It was the first time all weekend that she'd seen Drew without Casey.

"Have a safe trip, Dad," Drew told his father as Trevor belted Henry in his doggie harness.

"You too. Be careful going back to Ruston."

"Umm..." Drew shifted his weight from foot to foot, a nervous grin spreading across his young, earnest face.

"Is there something else?" Trevor asked his son as the three of them stood on the passenger side of his truck.

Drew turned to Jane. "Mrs. Lafitte, I want to propose to Casey if you'll allow it."

"Oh, my." Taken aback, Jane splayed a palm over her chest. She certainly hadn't expected this. Not so soon.

"I wanted to ask your permission. Do this right."

"I-I..." She shot a glance at Trevor who didn't look surprised.

"May I have your blessing?" Drew pressed his palms together.

"I didn't realize you were ready for this step."

Drew bit his bottom lip. "You think I'm jumping the gun?"

"Well..." She shot another look at Trevor.

He shrugged.

Fat lot of help he was. "You're a wonderful young man, Drew, and I can tell Casey really cares about you, but don't you think this is moving a little fast?"

Drew's face fell, and she felt cruddy for dashing his hopes. "We would have a long engagement. We do have to finish school first. We probably would not get married until next year."

What a relief that he considered education their priority.

"Please," Drew said. "I love her so much."

Who was she to stand in the way of true love?

Besides, they were grown adults and there was nothing she could do to stop them even if she wanted to. Even though she understood all the things that could go wrong, Jane nodded.

"You have my blessing."

Drew lit up with happiness and he spontaneously hugged Jane. His enthusiasm was endearing. "Thank you. I'm sorry to spring it on you like that, but your approval means a lot. I'm so happy you're on board."

"When do you plan on asking her?" Jane asked.

"I was hoping we could all go to Christmas Beach as soon as the semester is over in two weeks. We've got a cottage there and it would be the perfect setting for a proposal."

Oh yes, Jane knew the Christmas Beach bungalow well. That's where Trevor had proposed to her over two decades ago, but Drew didn't know that. It felt strange, thinking how her daughter and Trevor's son were following in their footsteps. She prayed the kids would have a much happier ending than she and Trevor had had.

"I would love that, Drew, and I think Casey would too."

"Of course, I'll be there." Trevor pulled his son into a bear hug.

"Well," Drew said, "I better get back to the house. Casey will be wondering where I got off to and I don't need her to get wind of this. I want it to be a complete surprise." With that, he turned and hurried back to the house, leaving Jane and Trevor alone once more.

"Wow," Jane said. "I did not see that coming so soon."

"Good thing we sorted ourselves out last night," he said.

"It is a good thing," she echoed.

"Guess I'll be seeing you in two weeks at Christmas Beach."

"Looks like it."

Trevor smiled, tipped his Stetson, and slid into his truck. As Jane watched him drive away, she couldn't help wondering what other memories and emotions would get stirred up on Christmas Beach.

NINE

Christmas

Beach

"What do you mean they're getting engaged?" Suzy scowled. "They've only been dating a few months."

Jane and Suzy had met at P.J.'s Coffee just around the block from Suzy's house for some post-weekend caffeine before starting work. Since the weather was moderate, they grabbed an outdoor table to people watch.

"I know, but they're adults. As difficult as it is for

me to accept, they get to make their own mistakes and I have to step back and let my kids lead their own lives." Jane reached for the creamer and poured a dollop into her coffee.

Might she and Trevor have repaired things if her parents had butted out of their romance? She loved her folks to pieces, and they were well meaning, but they'd had a hand in villainizing Trevor for going to Europe. They'd fueled Jane's hurt and outrage without offering a counterpoint or playing devil's advocate. They'd done what they thought best.

How would her parents react when they learned Casey was engaged to Trevor's son? *Yikes.* That wouldn't be fun, but she'd worry about it later.

"This is a delicate situation," Suzy said. "Things are complicated with you and Trevor."

She studied her friend. Because of her loyalty and devotion to Jane, Suzy had a hand in cast Trevor in the bad guy role as well.

Not that Jane was blaming her. Suzy had been her main support system during those awful days. Jane was just acknowledging a fact. She was also not letting herself off the hook. She'd been immature and in the throes of grief over Chad, and she'd reacted badly. Not an excuse for hardening her heart against

Trevor for deciding on a course she disagreed with, just a reason.

"Trevor and I had a long talk on Saturday night after dinner and we sorted out the past. I think it will be all right."

"Really?" Suzy's eyebrows went up.

"You gave me some sound advice at Pascal's, and I decided to take it."

"Well..." Suzy looked pleased with herself. "Glad I could help."

Talking about Trevor made Jane miss him—his laugh, the way he smelled, his deep sexy voice.

"So our little Casey is getting married." Suzy sighed. "They *do* grow up fast."

"They won't have a wedding for a least a year, so we've got plenty of time to help her plan even if we are the midst of the Harlow house reno."

"Oh boy." Suzy rubbed her palms together. "I can't wait."

"You old softie you." Jane lightly swatted her friend's shoulder. "Now, how about we get down to work?"

For Trevor, the next two weeks passed at a crawl as he looked forward to seeing Jane again at Christmas Beach.

The talk they'd had on her front porch swing sent his hopes soaring. He wouldn't do anything to impede his son's happiness or steal the limelight from Drew's proposal, but when the time was right, he couldn't help wishing something might develop between him and Jane.

Slow down, Doc. Love takes time.

Love.

Yes, he was falling in love all over again and it scared the living dickens out of him, even as it gave his heart wings.

On the day after Drew got home for winter break, they packed up the truck and headed to Christmas Beach. For two days, they cleaned and spruced up the cabin. It had been closed up since Labor Day and needed a little TLC before Jane and her children arrived.

That morning, they'd gone to the grocery store to stock up, and then they went fishing. Their guests were due to arrive around four in the afternoon. Trevor had tonight's dinner planned, with some freshly caught redfish, fileted and ready to grill. He would serve the fish with a huge pan of homemade au gratin potatoes and a fresh salad.

He wasn't much of a cook, but since Laura's passing, Trevor had grown his culinary repertoire beyond his prior scrambled eggs and Hamburger Helper. He knew how to grill, so that helped.

Christmas Beach was a small beach community at the tip of Louisiana on the Gulf Coast. Hurricane winds walloped the town every few years, but it always bounced back. Fortunately, the island was only two hours from New Orleans, so the drive for Jane and her family wasn't too arduous.

Drew planned to propose to Casey on the beach after dinner, so they set up tiki torches to light in the evening. Trevor also brought along his professional grade camera to record the proposal.

Just before four, Trevor noticed a car coming up the sandy drive, kicking up the usual white cloud of dust.

Jane.

His heart hammered.

Calm down.

This weekend was about Drew and Casey. He and Jane had plenty of time later for something to bloom if it was going to.

Casey jumped from the car before her mother

even put it in park and came running up the front porch steps and Drew flung himself out the door and into her arms.

Trevor grinned. He loved seeing his son so happy.

They helped unloaded the luggage and carried the suitcases into the cabin. Once everyone was settled, they headed back outside to enjoy the temperate evening.

"I'd forgotten how beautiful it was out here." Jane inhaled deeply the salty sea air and wrapped her thick cable-knit sweater more tightly around her. "I've missed this."

"When were you ever on Christmas Beach, Mom?" Casey asked.

Jane grimaced and blithely waved away her daughter's question. "Oh, back in college."

This was something he and Jane needed to talk about. When and how they would reveal their past to their children. As fast as things were moving between Drew and Casey, the sooner the better, but they didn't want to upstage Drew's proposal.

"Hey, c'mon," Drew said to Jason and Casey. "I want to show you guys the pier."

The three of them took off, leaving Trevor and Jane alone.

"Oops," Jane said when the kids were out of earshot. "I almost gave myself away." The cold ocean breeze blew her blond hair back from her face and the lowering sun cast a soft glow over her features. In that moment, she looked twenty-five. "The place is the same as it ever was."

Trevor felt as if they'd captured time in a bottle, all wind-blown and natural. "Thanks. Drew and I still drive down here and do some fishing whenever we can. Which granted, isn't often enough. I suppose that'll all change now that he and Casey will be engaged."

Jane angled him a look. "Yes, things are about to change in a big way."

"But good change," he said.

She smiled and tucked an errant strand of hair behind a delicate ear. "The best kind."

Trevor cleared his throat. There was something he needed to prepare Jane for. "Just so you know, I've given Drew Laura's wedding ring to propose to Casey with. I hope that's okay with you."

"Why would I care?" she asked, looking surprised.

"Because it was my grandmother's ring."

Jane sucked in her breath, and he could tell she

was struggling to keep her expression noncommittal. "I see."

It was the same ring Trevor had given Jane when he'd asked her to marry him. The same ring she'd quickly given back to him when he told her he accepted the European internship. They'd been engaged for literally all of ten minutes.

"Laura wanted Drew's bride to have it." Trevor clenched his jaw as tension ran through his body. This was a touchy subject.

"Did Laura know you'd once given the ring to another woman?"

"I told her about you, yes." He paused. "Did you tell David about me?"

"I did."

"So neither of us kept secrets from our spouses."

"That's good, right? How does Drew feel about Laura's ring? I'm assuming he doesn't know the full history."

Her empathy for his son touched Trevor's heart. "It's a family heirloom, and he feels honored to give it to Casey."

"It *is* a lovely ring," she said. "I'm glad he's giving it to her."

"You don't mind?"

"It's not about me, Trevor. The kids and their

happiness are what's important, and it really is a magnificent ring. Casey will be thrilled..." She paused. "Just as I was."

For all of ten minutes until he'd ruined everything. "Thank you for being so understanding."

He smiled at her. She had grown from that passionate young woman who took everything to heart into a measured, mature adult who could see all sides of things. He hoped he'd grown and changed as much as Jane had.

"But of course." Her returning smile tugged at his heartstrings.

"I'm going inside to get dinner ready," he said.

She rubbed her palms together. "Tell me what I can do to help."

They went inside and together prepped dinner. Trevor took out the fish filets for grilling, while Jane tossed a garden salad.

"Oh, I snuck in some flowers while Casey wasn't looking. Let me go grab them from the trunk." She hurried off.

From the kitchen window, Trevor could see Casey, Drew, and Jason out on the beach, barefooted, their pants legs rolled up to the knees, playing in the surf like children. He was certain the water must be freezing by now, so he lit the kindling and added logs to the fireplace in the family room.

Jane came back inside carrying a large bouquet of white flowers. "Here we go."

"Those smell nice."

"They're camellias from my yard."

"Beautiful," he said, but he wasn't talking about the flowers. Instead, his gazed fixed on Jane's smiling face and her lively green eyes.

"Thanks." Her cheeks pinked, and she ducked her head as she went about arranging the flowers.

"When do you think we should tell the kids about us?" he asked, setting the table.

"Not this weekend. We don't want to take the spotlight off Casey and Drew."

"Agreed," he said. "But soon?"

"And when we do, maybe we should leave out that you asked me to marry you right here on Christmas Beach and that you gave me the ring Drew will now be giving Casey. It's just too complicated."

"I agree," he said. "They don't need to know all the gory details."

"We don't want to detract from their happiness."

"No."

"Deal?" She stuck out her hand.

"Deal." Trevor shook it, still wondering if they

were making a mistake by keeping their past relationship under wraps for a while longer.

How would Drew and Casey react when they finally found out?

..*.*.*.*.*.*.*.*.

Jane was hanging on by a thread.

Learning that Casey would wear the same ring Trevor had given Jane took her breath away. It had been a quarter of a century, so why should she still care? And being here at the same beach house where she and Trevor had made memories together—it felt like she'd been sucked back in time while simultaneously thrust into new waters. She busied herself snipping stems and arranging flowers, which relaxed her a bit and drew attention away from their conversation.

Trevor prepared the fish for grilling with butter, minced garlic, sliced lemon, and parmesan. He had already slipped a big pan of sliced potatoes into the oven before he'd started the fish.

"Hungry?" he asked.

"Starved." Maybe food was what she needed to

get her emotions in check. Low blood sugar affected her mood.

Trevor filled a wineglass with an oaken chardonnay and set it on the counter in front of where she perched on a high barstool.

"Thank you." She took an appreciative sniff and swirled the liquid gently. "This smells like apples."

"It's from a winery in Texas." He then pulled out a small platter of crackers and shrimp dip from the refrigerator. "As an appetizer."

His thoughtfulness charmed her and reminded Jane why she'd been so crazy about him in the first place. Who was she kidding? Jane hadn't ever gotten over him completely, which was why this was so difficult.

At dinner, the five of them sat together around the kitchen table, laughing and talking. Jane was pleased by how comfortable they'd all become with one another in such a brief time. When they'd finished eating, everyone cleared their plates from the table, led by Drew, who was eager to hurry things along.

Once the kitchen was clean, Trevor suggested they go outside onto the deck at sunset. He was ready with his high-end camera. Jane was glad he'd thought to bring it.

Drew led Casey over to the deck's weathered railing—a perfect spot that overlooked the sandy beach and crashing waves below. The sun was just slipping down the horizon, casting a warm golden glow across the water. Casey gasped in delighted surprise as Drew got down on one knee, the breeze catching her long blond hair.

"Casey Lafitte, from the moment I met you I knew you were the one for me," Drew began.

Jane watched her daughter tremble as Casey realized what was happening, and Jane recalled her own similar reaction to Trevor's proposal. She glanced over at him, but he was busy videotaping the proposal and she couldn't gauge his reaction.

"Your smile lights up any room you walk into."

Casey's hands flew to cover her mouth.

"Your joy and passion for life are infectious. You make me want to be a better person every single day," Drew gazed up at Casey with pure love in his eyes.

Joyful tears pooled in her bright-blue eyes. Drew took out a small velvet box and opened it to reveal the glittering two-carat diamond ring that Jane remembered well. "Will you make me the happiest man in the world and marry me?"

"Yes! Of course I'll marry you!" Casey exclaimed, laughing and crying at the same time.

Drew slipped the ring onto the third finger of her left hand. He stood up and hugged her, the two of them swept away in a cocoon of love and happiness.

The beautiful scene unfolding on the deck pushed complicated emotions into Jane's throat. Tears threatened to spill from her own eyes. The pure elation on her daughter's face as she admired the dazzling ring on her finger was everything Jane had hoped for from this sweet proposal. Seeing Casey so full of joy made keeping the secret of her relationship with Trevor worthwhile. There was plenty of time to tell them later.

This special moment should be savored.

Jane hadn't seen Casey this happy since before her father passed away. Back when life was simple and uncomplicated. Jane wished she could freeze this moment forever. She tried to commit every detail to memory—the sound of the crashing waves, the salty sea air, Casey's melodic laugh as she excitedly told Drew how surprised she'd been by his unexpected proposal, but how overjoyed he'd popped the question and at such a magical place.

Trevor came up behind Jane and squeezed her shoulder in congratulations.

Jane turned and gave him a teary smile, dabbing

at her eyes with a tissue. She hadn't expected to get so emotional, but this day meant the world. She was so proud of the woman Casey had become and so thrilled for her daughter's future with Drew, who was already like a son to Jane.

After a few more blissful moments admiring her new ring, Casey turned and ran over to Jane, throwing her arms around her in a warm embrace.

"Mom, can you believe this? I had no idea!" Casey proudly held out her hand to show off the sparkling diamond.

"It's stunning, sweetie. I'm just so happy for you," Jane said, hugging her daughter tight.

"Congratulations, you two." Trevor shook Drew's hand before pulling him into a fatherly hug.

Jason also congratulated his sister and her groom-to-be.

They popped open a bottle of champagne and toasted the newly engaged couple as twilight fell over the ocean. Laughter and joy filled the beach house as Casey and Drew recounted the proposal story again and again.

It was a perfect evening, but Jane couldn't ignore the bittersweet ache in her heart. Seeing the young love between Casey and Drew juxtaposed with her own life brought up a flood of nostalgia.

She caught Trevor staring at her several times throughout the night with a deep longing in his eyes that made her blush and turn away. Her feelings were so intense, she couldn't let herself get swept away.

Jane tried to push the conflicting thoughts out of her head and focus on celebrating Casey and Drew. There would be time to deal with her complicated history with Trevor later. Tonight was about new beginnings.

Casey raised her champagne flute, her cheeks flushed with happiness. "To an amazing night with the people I love most!"

They clinked glasses again.

Jane pulled her into another tight hug, whispering into her ear, "I love you so much."

No matter what happened next, Jane would always cherish this golden evening celebrating her daughter finding a life partner. She said a silent prayer of thanks for this great blessing, even if it did mean tying herself to Trevor forever.

Or maybe that was part of her joy.

TEN

After Jane and her kids left on Sunday morning, Trevor prowled the beach cottage.

He couldn't seem to sit still. He and Jane were going to be in-laws, and he had to face that. They would see each other for birthdays, holiday celebrations, and the big events in their children's lives. No way around it.

Their heart-to-heart back in New Orleans had peeled back the old layers. Laid bare the hurt and while their visit on Christmas Beach had been amiable, the wounds felt as fresh as ever.

Jane was still leery of him. He could see suspicion in her eyes. He didn't know if she could ever truly forgive him, and he didn't blame her.

He'd destroyed her belief in him when he'd left for Europe. The timing of his leaving hadn't been ideal and if he hadn't been so bent on seeing the world, he and Jane might've worked things out. But if they'd worked it out, he wouldn't have met Laura. Wouldn't have his son. So how could he regret it?

"Everything okay, Dad?" Drew finished rinsing their breakfast dishes in the sink and dried his hands on a kitchen towel. "You keep pacing around and staring out the window as if it holds the answer to an ancient secret."

"Yes, I'm fine. Just been thinking about how much your mom would've loved helping plan your wedding." Of course, this was true, so Trevor didn't feel as guilty as he would've had he outright lied to his son, but it was a partial truth at best.

Drew's mouth tugged down and his face softened. "I know."

"She would be so proud of you."

"I know that too."

"She would love Casey to pieces."

Drew gave a faint smile. "You really think so?"

"Yes."

"I think she would have liked Jane too, don't you?" Drew arched an eyebrow.

Wow, what a complicated thought. Trevor skirted it and put on a bright smile of his own. "Do you want to go fishing?"

"Are you changing the topic?"

"I am."

"Do you like Jane?" Drew asked point-blank.

This would have been the perfect time to tell his son about his past relationship with Jane. But he didn't want to do that without Jane's permission or without Casey around. He and Jane were in this subterfuge together.

"Jane's a nice woman." He kept emotion out of his tone.

"She's beautiful," Drew said. "It's where Casey gets her looks."

"You're right. Do you want to fish off the pier or rent a boat?"

"Too cold for a boat. What are we fishing for today?"

"Crappie?" Trevor loved the white perch also

known as sac-a-lait. Crappie was a mild white fish that tasted delicious no matter how it was prepared. He liked that crappie had a similar texture and flavor to tilapia, without the questionable farming methods.

"Yeah. Crappie fishing is fun."

They'd rigged their fishing rods and reels with the proper hooks, sinkers, and bait, whistled to Henry to come along, and the three of them headed down to the dock.

Sitting in camp chairs, they chatted about sports and Drew's courses at school as they reeled in crappie after crappie. Trevor had baited the waters under the dock with last year's Christmas tree. The old tree attracted the crappie who enjoyed hiding in the sheltering branches. His dad had taught him the technique, and he was passing it on to his son. The Christmas trees set up a food chain. Algae grew in the branches and microorganisms were attracted to the algae. Baitfish moved in to feed on the plankton and that lured in the game fish like crappie.

Fishing with his son was everything to Trevor— and he selfishly wondered how much they would get to fish together once Drew and Casey were married.

Trevor rarely allowed himself the luxury of

moping or marinating in gloom, but he wasn't as ready for this transition in their lives as he'd believed. The thought of sharing his only son with somebody else was unsettling.

Not that he didn't like Casey—in fact, he was well on his way to loving her like the daughter he'd never had—especially since she was Jane's child. Change was hard, though, and he wanted to hold on to his little boy as long as possible.

And then it occurred to him that one day, in the not too distance future, he could have a grandchild to fish with and Trevor grinned. Hot dog, now that would be something!

"Hey, Dad, would you mind if we went to New Orleans? I want to buy Casey a Christmas gift." His voice when up and he gnawed on his bottom lip. Was he worried Trevor would get upset?

They normally hung around the camp and happily fished, watched old movies, and played video games, just enjoying their time together. But he seemed distracted, and Trevor felt antsy, so maybe a change of scenery would help.

"Okay, let's go Christmas shopping. I haven't shopped for Aunt JuJu or your grandparents yet."

Drew grinned. "Thanks, Dad."

Trevor gave his shoulder a quick squeeze. "Maybe we could see Casey and Jane. Take them to dinner."

"That'd be great!" Drew's eyes brightened and Trevor felt his own spirits lift.

Within an hour, they packed up their clothes, locked up the cottage, and were headed for New Orleans.

:★*:*★*:*★*:*★*:*★*:*

Jane and Suzy were doing an initial walk-through with their favorite contractor, Desmond. They would measure, plan, and schedule the demolition on the new renovation project. They were still waiting for approval from the city and its many permits, including the Certificate of Appropriateness from the Historic District Landmarks Commission. This process usually took as long to clear as building permits. It gave Jane and Suzy time to do all the pre-planning that didn't physically affect the structure.

They wore hard hats and work boots to avoid nails, glass, and other possible hazards in the old unoccupied structure as they stepped inside the front door. As they discussed the stained-glass transom window above the front door, Jane noticed an old blue pickup pull into the driveway.

Her pulse ticked. What was Trevor doing back in New Orleans?

"Excuse me." Jane stepped off the front porch and approached the truck.

"Hi, Mrs. Lafitte." Drew greeted her, leaning over the seat to wave across Henry and Trevor.

"Hello, Drew." She sought Trevor's gaze and held it. "What are y'all doing back in town so soon? I thought you were staying at the beach until Christmas Eve."

"We decided to do some holiday shopping. We're behind with our list." Trevor grinned at her from behind a pair of Wayfarers. He wore a blue-and-white striped flannel shirt and had a slight shadow on his jaw.

Had he forgotten to shave, or was he growing a beard? Either way, the stubble was downright sexy. Which she should not be noticing. Why did her body go all soft and warm at the sight of this man? She wasn't twenty-five years old anymore.

"Where are y'all staying in town?" she asked, far happier to see them than she should have been.

"With my parents and we were driving through

the neighborhood on our way there. I remembered you and Suzy were renovating the house and I wanted to show it to Drew since he's an engineering major and loves these old homes. I hope that's okay."

Was that the only reason Trevor had dropped by? Architecture?

"We're just finishing up with our contractor, so y'all can come in and have a look around. But be super careful because there's broken glass and nails scattered everywhere."

"Great. Thanks so much."

Jane spent some time showing them what they had planned for the house. When they were done, they invited her and Casey out to dinner. Instead, she invited them to her house. "I'll make muffulettas."

"Sounds fantastic," Trevor said.

"See you at seven?"

"We'll be there," Drew said.

By the time the Gardner men drove away, both Suzy and Desmond were gone. Being around Trevor and pretending not to know him was exhausting. They needed to tell the kids who they were sooner rather than later. Jane hated keeping secrets. Maybe they could do it tonight. Hopefully, the kids wouldn't be too upset that they hadn't come clean in the first place.

Jane headed home, just now realizing she'd been with Trevor wearing work boots and safety gear. Gracious, she must look a sight.

As Jane drove, she gnawed on her lip a little. She was anxious about seeing Trevor again, of course, but she was also worried about something else.

Jane was considering selling her home but hadn't mentioned it to her children yet because she still wasn't sure. The house was large and worth far more than she had in it, including the renovations they'd done over the years. This recent seller's market might not come around again for a while. But selling the house meant risking upsetting her kids. They'd grown up here, and all their memories with their father were wrapped up in this house.

Of course, she most likely wouldn't put it on the market before the wedding, depending on when that would be. Casey and Drew claimed they'd wait at least a year, but Jane worried they wouldn't wait that long.

Casey met her at the door. "Drew texted me you'd invited him and his dad to dinner. That was so sweet of you. Thanks, Mom."

"Then you won't mind giving me a hand with the muffulettas."

"Mind? Heck, I'm so excited, I'll make the whole dinner while you relax, put up your feet, and have a glass of wine."

"That's sounds wonderful."

"Oh, and Mom?"

"Uh-huh?" Jane asked, hanging up her jacket on the coatrack near the front door.

"Can we invite Drew and his dad to Christmas?"

Wow, she didn't know if she was quite ready to share Christmas with Trevor. The thought of sitting across from Trevor for Christmas dinner right now was a little much. Things were changing, and she was struggling to keep up. But Drew and Casey were engaged; of course her daughter wanted to spend time with Drew over Christmas.

"Mmm, I hadn't planned on company."

"Please." Casey pressed her palms together.

"Okay, I guess. Y'all work it out."

"Yay! Thank you."

"Just remember that we'll be with your grandparents at their house on Christmas Eve," Jane said.

Christmas Eve with her folks was a hard and fast tradition and they'd never deviated, not even once.

"I know."

"And keep in mind that Trevor and Drew have their own family traditions as well."

"What if they invite me to go over to their house on Christmas Eve?" Casey asked.

"Then you'll have a decision to make." Jane thought about Trevor's parents who lived near the Harlow house.

The Gardners were lovely folks, and she knew they would treat Casey well. But yikes, they were bound to bring up Jane's relationship with Trevor. She and Trevor needed to get out in front of this. She'd pull him aside tonight to discuss the timing of their confession.

She left Casey making muffulettas and went upstairs for a shower and change of clothes. She came back down to the sounds of male voices. Trevor and Drew were here.

Jane found them in the family room. Drew and Casey were standing close to each other, chattering up a storm. Jason was slouched on the couch, scrolling on his phone. Henry was sprawled out on the rug in front of the fireplace.

And Trevor was holding a white box with a pink ribbon from a popular bakery near the French quarter that made the loveliest cakes.

His eyes lit up when he spied her, and she wished

she'd put on something nicer than jeans and a sweatshirt.

"It's a yule log," Trevor explained and extended the box to Jane. "We couldn't come to dinner empty-handed."

"That was sweet of you, thanks." She accepted the bakery box and carried it into the kitchen.

Trevor followed.

Drew and Casey were within earshot.

"Could I speak to you outside on the deck?" she asked him.

"Sure." Jamming his hands into his front pockets, Trevor followed her to the backyard.

Jane closed the door and glanced over her shoulder to make sure the kids hadn't followed them. "We need to tell the kids about our past. Casey wants to spend Christmas with Drew and if they're around our parents, it's bound to come up that you and I were once hot and heavy."

"We could ask them to keep quiet."

"That's not fair to them or our kids."

He nodded, hunching his shoulders against the cool breeze blowing through the trees and scattering leaves across the yard. "They are all three here, let's just do it."

"Okay." Jane squared her shoulders and blew out

her breath. There were bound to be questions she wasn't sure if she was ready to answer, but it was time to come clean.

Once everyone was seated around the table about to dig into their sandwiches, Trevor and Jane exchanged a look. She nodded at him. Go time.

He cleared his throat. "Kids, we've got something to tell you."

All three young people swung their gaze to the end of table where Trevor was seated. The same spot where David used to sit.

Jane felt a twinge of nostalgia and loss. She rested her palms flat against the table and gave Trevor her attention as well.

"Jane and I..." He paused.

"Dad, are you about to tell us you guys dating?" Drew asked, his eyes twinkling with delight.

"No, no," Jane said. "Not that. Not that at all."

"But we *did* date," Trevor said. "Once upon a time. In fact, we were even engaged briefly."

Jane studied her son and daughter's faces, bracing herself for the fallout. But instead of looking alarmed or surprised, Casey grinned, and Jason nibbled a potato chip.

Drew shrugged. "We know."

"You know?" Trevor blinked.

"How?" Jane asked.

"Mom," Casey said. "At college, Drew and I were in the library, and we saw they had college yearbooks on the shelf. We looked you up and found a picture of you and Trevor. In the photograph, Drew's dad had his arm around your shoulders and from the expressions on your faces, it was clear you were pretty into each other. I took a snapshot of the photo and showed it to Jason. We decided to stay mum."

"So you knew all along about Trevor and me?" Jane shook her head. "Why didn't you say anything?"

"We figured whatever happened to you back then was none of our business," Drew said.

"Yeah." Jason nodded. "We've done our best to stay out of your way so you two could reconnect."

"We hate that you've been so lonely since Dad died," Casey added.

Wow. Jane stared at her kids. They were even more mature than she thought they were.

"So you've been what?" Trevor asked. "Matchmaking?"

"Not matchmaking exactly," Drew said. "Just giving y'all space to figure things out."

What? Jane couldn't believe it. All this time that the kids had left Jane and Trevor alone, she had no idea they were purposely giving them space to sort out their baggage.

"So now," Casey said, "you don't have to keep pretending you don't know each other. If you want to date again, go for it! You have our blessings!"

ELEVEN

"Can you believe our audacious kids?" Jane asked after the three young people shooed them out of the kitchen, insisting they would wash the dinner dishes. "Keeping quiet that they knew we had a past and trying to play matchmaker."

Taking Henry for a walk, they strolled Napoleon Avenue, taking in the splendor of the houses aglow with Christmas lights.

"No," Trevor said. "But I'm glad it's all out in the open. No more secrets."

"Me too, but I wished they'd told us from the beginning that they knew."

"To ease your mind, we don't have to date or anything just because they were trying to play matchmaker." He slanted her a long look. "No reason to feel obligated."

"I know," she said.

"Although I wouldn't be opposed to it," he murmured.

Jane shook her head. "I'm just not ready for that."

"I get it," he said. "I hurt you badly back then. I understand if a second chance isn't in the cards for us."

"It's enough that we can be civil," she said. "Now that we're going to be in-laws. I'm happy with that."

"We can start with friendship." Trevor smiled.

"I'd like that." Jane raised the collar on her jacket as the wind kicked up.

"What do you think your parents will say when they find out Drew is my son?"

"Momma might be prickly. She sure was upset

with you when you broke my heart," Jane said. "But she'll sort herself out."

"I completely understand. I deserve her scorn, but I'll do my best to win her over."

"You raised a wonderful son in Drew, and that will go a long way in winning Momma's heart." Jane smiled.

"You did the same with your children," he said. "Casey is a lovely young woman, and I know Drew really likes Jason as well."

He looked up at the sky, which darkened with thick clouds as night fell. "We should head back."

Jane nodded, and they turned to walk home. They were both silent, but it was a comfortable silence that spoke of understanding and forgiveness.

And Jane realized with a start, she was more at peace than she'd been in a very long time.

✨★✨★✨★✨★✨★✨

It was Christmas Eve, and Trevor and Drew were back in New Orleans. They'd celebrated an early Christmas dinner with Aunt Julie and her family in

Lafayette before heading back so that Casey and Drew could spend their first Christmas together as a couple. Julie had been disappointed over their absence from Christmas Day festivities on the farm but supported Drew's wish to be with his beloved.

Julie offered to keep Henry at the farm during their trip, but both Trevor and Drew wanted the old hound dog with them for the holidays. Henry snored between them as they made the now familiar drive up Napoleon Avenue toward Jane's house. Drew had bathed his best buddy with a floral-scented shampoo so he would be extra lovable.

Trevor was excited to see the Lafittes, as he considered them to be part of his family now—despite their peculiar situation.

When they arrived at Jane's house, Henry perked up and gave a howl of pleasure. Despite their questionable beginning, he and Jane were becoming fast friends and for now, it was enough.

In the back of his pickup, they'd loaded all the gifts in a large heavy-duty trash bag, not wanting to risk them getting wet in case of rain. It wasn't unusual for South Louisiana to get a shower with little warning, even in the dead of winter.

Trevor drove into the driveway and spotted Jane

sitting on the front porch swing, wearing reading glasses and a puffy jacket, working on her laptop. As a successful business owner, she spent a considerable amount of time working. He admired her for holding everything together the way she had after losing her husband. Knowing how hard that was, Trevor related to those challenges.

He noted the huge wreath on the front door and all the small seasonal accents that made her house so welcoming. Weirdly, he felt a sense of coming home whenever he was here. She raised a hand and waved as soon as she saw them, then stood up and stepped off the porch.

Once they'd parked, Trevor and Drew grabbed their belongings and headed toward the front of the house to greet her.

Putting down his load, Drew ran over and gave her a big hug, which warmed Trevor's heart. The two of them had already formed a bond. Trevor was uncertain how exactly to greet Jane, so he did what most people in this part of the country did when greeting a close friend or relative.

He kissed her cheek. "Merry Christmas, Jane."

She flushed prettily, and he caught a whiff of her sugar-cookie scent. "Merry Christmas."

"We're glad y'all could make it," she said.

Before Trevor could reply, Henry whined at Jane, waiting for his greeting.

"Hello, big guy. Merry Christmas to you too." She bent down and dropped a kiss on top of Henry's head.

Once inside, Casey offered them hot cocoa with marshmallows and a plate of home-baked cookies. Trevor had missed these small touches in his life over the past few years. Laura had always baked during the holidays.

"We're due at Momma and Daddy's in half an hour for dinner if you'd like to freshen up before we go, and Henry has been invited to join us since it's Christmas."

Trevor frowned at the dog. "Are you sure?"

"It was Momma's idea, so if things go wonky, it's on her."

"No kidding?"

"She was pretty even keel when she learned you were Drew's dad and that you and I had made amends. I think she wants to make amends too. It's probably for Casey's sake rather than yours, but I say we take what we can get." Jane laughed.

Jane's mother could be a little rigid, so he was glad to hear that she'd softened toward him.

"That sounds great."

"You sure you're ready for this?" Jane asked.

"Absolutely," Trevor said and meant it.

::*:*:*:*:*:*:*:*:*:*

Christmas Eve at Jane's family leaned toward the traditional. Jane brought her home-baked goodies to dinner. Momma had outdone herself with the standing rib roast, fingerling potatoes, and haricots verts, as she liked to call the green beans. The home-made yeast rolls had taken two days to make as Momma made a point of telling everyone, more than once.

After dinner, the family gathered around the enormous Christmas tree to open gifts. Trevor surprised Jane by handing a wrapped package to both her parents from him and Drew. Momma loved Christmas Eve and giving gifts.

Trevor's eyes widened as Momma handed him a wrapped present. "You got me something?"

"You're a guest in my home," Momma said. "And you're about to become an in-law. Of course I did."

"Thank you so much."

Momma looked pleased with herself. "You're welcome."

Trevor opened the package to find a hand-knitted scarf in a color of blue that perfectly matched his eyes. "Thank you, Mrs. Theriot. It's very soft. What a generous gift. I truly appreciate it."

Jane studied her mother's face and to her surprise, Momma actually smiled at him. "You're so very welcome."

Wow. Jane stared at her mother. Trevor had survived the gauntlet. Even Momma was willing to let go of her anger.

Hope filled her heart. Maybe, just maybe, she and Trevor could actually find their way back to each other. It wouldn't be easy, and it would take time, but it was a growing dream she couldn't deny.

✦✦✦✦✦✦✦✦✦✦✦✦

On Christmas morning at her house, after breakfast had been eaten and the presents opened, Jane sat on the plush sofa next to Trevor in front of the crackling fire, sipping hot cocoa with Henry at their feet.

She'd gotten Trevor a box of chocolates as a gift,

something delicious, but that didn't say they were anything more than friends. He'd been equally circumspect in his gift giving, buying her a pair of warm fuzzy booties. She wore them now, her feet propped up on the ottoman.

Drew, Casey, and Jason had gone caroling at the Children's Hospital with a group from their church, leaving her all alone in the house with Trevor. Suzy was coming over in the afternoon, bringing her famous Christmas lasagna for their evening meal.

"You look so relaxed," he said, delight flickering in those fathomless blue eyes. "I missed seeing you like this."

She drank in the sight of him. He was dressed casually in gray sweatpants, house slippers, and a faded chambray shirt with the top two buttons undone and the sleeves rolled up to his elbows. His hair was mussed, the blond strands threaded with silver. He smiled tentatively. The expression placed a slight dimple in his left cheek.

"I *feel* at ease," Jane said so softly she could barely hear herself speak. She raised her gaze and met his eyes head-on.

He turned toward her on the couch, trying to appear nonchalant, but the way he looked at her gave him away. He was nervous.

Hmmm.

"I'm happy for our kids," he said.

"Me too." She wondered what he was getting at.

"Seeing them so much in love reminds me so much of what we once had."

"Me too," she echoed. "I wish we'd had staying power back then."

"I'm here now, Jane." His voice deepened and his blue eyes turned tender.

Yes, he was.

She raked her gaze over him, appreciating the ways he'd changed. Not just physically, but emotionally, too. She could only hope she'd grown as much as he had, becoming a better person with the progressing years.

"Yes." She didn't know what else to say. Jane worried a stray thread on the sleeve of her sweater, suddenly feeling exposed. Vulnerable. But also grateful to Trevor for his reassurance. His coming for Christmas was a soothing balm for her soul.

Trevor straightened on the couch. "I know the past few weeks have been bumpy. But challenges either break you or strengthen you. And I believe we have a real opportunity here for growth, if we're brave enough to take it."

Jane stilled, pulse thrumming, and she hitched in her breath. "What kind of opportunity?"

Trevor scooted closer. His handsome face was solemn, his eyes twin blue flames. "A second chance, Jane. I lost you once because I was young and foolish. I'll always regret letting you go." His voice dropped lower. "Truth be told, no matter how happy I was with Laura, I never really stopped loving you."

Jane's head swam. The room seemed to fall away as his words echoed through a timeless void. She felt the same way. She'd loved David with all her heart, but there had been no one like Trevor.

He went on, his tone earnest. "I know we can't ignore the past, but when I saw you again, all the old feelings came tumbling back. Feelings I'd pushed aside and forgot about for twenty-five years. I don't want to make that mistake again."

Jane knotted her hands in her lap to steady herself, complex emotions swirling through her— joy, fear, hope, uncertainty.

"What are you saying?" she whispered.

"I'm saying I'd like us to try again, Jane. A fresh start. If you're willing to take a chance on me." His eyes locked intensely on hers.

Jane's pulse pounded, heat flooding her cheeks despite the December chill. She saw nothing but raw honesty in Trevor's steady gaze. Still, uncertainties clouded her mind. "I don't want either of us to get hurt again."

"I know." Trevor ran a hand through his hair. "Believe me, I've played through every worst-case scenario in my mind a thousand times, but staying apart out of fear we could end isn't really living."

He closed the small distance between them to rest his arm on the back of the couch behind Jane's body. She drew in another shaky breath, acutely aware of his nearness. His woodsy cologne stirred poignant memories.

"Jane." Her name was a fervent prayer on his lips. "We've been given a second chance to make things right and now we know our kids and our parents all approve of us being together again. Don't let past regrets rob us of a future. I want to date you. I want to see where this could lead."

His impassioned words resonated through Jane, cracking the walls around her heart. He was right. They had something special. It was worth the risk.

Jane met his searching gaze. "A fresh start would be a dream come true, but let's take things slowly."

Relief broke across Trevor's face. His hand slid to cover Jane's. "Slow works for me, as long we keep moving forward. I'll wait as long as it takes. I'll prove to you that this time, your trust in me won't be misplaced."

Moved by the sincerity in his voice, Jane turned her palm up to link their fingers. "Okay then. We're really doing this?"

Trevor exhaled and smiled, his eyes crinkling at the corners. "Yeah, we really are."

Their joined hands formed a tentative commitment. After so many years, they'd found their way back to each other.

It felt like destiny.

He leaned in and she swore he was going to kiss her, when a knock rapped on the front door, followed by the door opening and Suzy hollering, "Yoo-hoo, anybody home?"

Henry whined and hopped to his feet.

"We're in here," Jane called.

Suzy sauntered in, carrying a pan of lasagna. "Oh," she said and stopped. "Don't you two look cozy."

Henry thumped his tail and rubbed against Trevor's leg.

"I'm gonna take Henry out for some air," Trevor said.

"Don't run off on account of me." Suzy winked.

Jane got up. "I wasn't expecting you until later."

"I finished the lasagna sooner than I thought. Used those no boil noodles this time, and it shaved twenty minutes off the prep."

"The kids are still caroling."

"Good. It'll give us a chance to chat." Suzy headed for the kitchen.

Jane was still feeling a little disoriented from what she'd been certain was about to their first kiss in twenty-five years until Suzy interrupted.

"I'm gonna walk Henry…" Trevor trailed off.

They lingered like teenagers in the hallway after class, both reluctant to part. The air between them shimmered with anticipation of what was to come.

Finally, Trevor went out the back door with his dog, leaving Jane nothing to do but follow her friend. In the kitchen, Jane blinked, breaking the spell of the emotionally charged moment.

Suzy's eyes widened. "What on earth has happened?"

Blinking back tears, Jane sagged against the wall. "Trevor wants to date."

"Why, that's wonderful news!" Suzy paused. "Isn't it?"

"Y-yes."

"So are these happy tears?" Suzy asked, plucking a clean tissue from her pocket and passing it to her.

"Uh-huh." Jane dabbed at her eyes. "Are you upset with me?"

"What for?"

"Crying like a big old baby."

"Are you kidding? After all the tears of grief you've cried over that man, I'm thrilled you're finally crying tears of joy!"

TWELVE

Over the course of the next year, Jane and Trevor took things slowly. Whenever he was in New Orleans for a consultation, he would call her for a date.

They had a wonderful time together getting to know each other all over again. They went to restaurants, attended concerts and plays, and they even braved the French Quarter for Mardi Gras.

For months, they did nothing more than hold

hands. They talked and talked and talked. Straightening out the past, learning what each other liked and disliked these days, planning the wedding, and imagining future grandkids.

For Casey and Drew's graduation in May, they drove to Ruston together and had a wonderful time. When Trevor dropped her off on her front porch afterward, they shared their first kiss, and it was glorious.

Better even than their very first kiss twenty-five years earlier.

Jane woke up each morning yearning to be with Trevor and went to bed at night with a smile on her face as each day just got better and better. They texted often and Trevor called her once a week on Friday evening, and they would chat into the wee hours of the morning.

During the summer, they spent time with the kids on Christmas Beach, all of them fishing together as they discussed the wedding. Both sets of parents joined them for the Fourth of July, and it was a mini reunion. Everyone got along so well Jane found it hard to believe there had once been so much animosity.

On the twenty-sixth anniversary of Chad's death, Jane and Trevor visited the cemetery together and left flowers. Jane couldn't help feeling her older brother would have been happy she and Trevor had reconnected. There had been too much death in their lives for them not to celebrate the precious moments.

Drew and Casey went back and forth on weekends between Lafayette and New Orleans, spending time with their families and each other. Drew's summer internship was in Lafayette at an architectural engineering firm, so he was there during the week. He'd applied for a job with the Corp of Engineers in New Orleans, which would start in the fall after his internship ended. Casey applied for several library and media center specialist positions throughout the city.

For Jane, wedding planning fell within her wheelhouse, and besides the time it took from her busy schedule, it didn't overwhelm her in the least. Most days after work, she spent a couple of hours researching and making lists with Casey.

Instead of searching venues in the city, Casey and Drew decided to marry at the site of their engagement, Trevor's beach house on Christmas Beach, and they wanted to get married at Christmas. Trevor seemed thrilled to host the wedding at his home. They'd texted back and forth, sharing ideas about the wedding and chitchatting about everyday kinds of things.

This made the wedding planning more manageable financially, but since the venue was out of town, it was more complicated. Everything would have to be driven over for setup. But they'd found a fantastic Cajun caterer in the town of Christmas Beach. The photographer could travel two and a half hours from New Orleans and was, fortunately, a friend of Jane's. Jane had planned the flowers and centerpieces herself.

In November, the renovation of the Harlow place was finally done, which gave Jane a breather to focus solely on the wedding. By the time December rolled around, everything was in place for the big event.

Jane met Trevor at the beach house with Casey and Jason the day before the wedding. She was impressed at how much work he'd done to get the house ready. There was an enormous Christmas tree in the family room decorated with white lights and gold and silver bows and ornaments. The Christmas wedding theme carried throughout the house.

"You've done an incredible job here." Jane complimented his efforts.

"I have to give most of the credit to Julie. She came down her last week and worked her magic."

"Please tell her how much I appreciate her time and efforts to make this wedding special for the kids."

"You can tell her yourself when you see her at the ceremony tomorrow."

"I will." Jane smiled at him, wishing there was time to say more, but she still had work to do before the wedding.

Jane could tell that Trevor wanted to talk to her, maybe say more, but with all the last-minute preparations going on around them, they didn't get the opportunity.

The next morning on Christmas Eve, the wedding photographer arrived, along with the caterers and hair and makeup stylists. Suzy also showed up early, which was a blessing to have her best friend on hand.

The florist delivered the flowers and together with Suzy, Jane quickly worked her magic on the red and white rose floral arrangements as the caterers set up. She arranged the rest of the flowers, including Casey's bouquet, the boutonnieres, and corsages for parents and grandparents. The florist came to set up an arch on the beach where the bride and groom would say their vows. Today's weather was stunning. The sun shone, and the temperature hovered in the low sixties, festive and pleasant.

Her mother and father had rented outdoor heaters to help the chill away after the sun went down. Jane stepped outside to make sure everything was going as planned. Trevor came up the deck stairs. He'd been out on the beach, helping Jason set up the chairs.

"Everyone has done an incredible job." Trevor surveyed the twinkle lights strung overhead and the floral centerpieces on the tables set with white table-cloths and sheer overlays for the reception. "It's breathtaking."

"I agree." She smiled at him.

"We haven't really talked since you got here," he said. "Are you doing okay?"

She gave him a thumbs-up. "Got a few butterflies in my stomach, but it's excitement more than nerves. I'm just so happy for our kids."

"Me too." He leaned in and she thought for a split second he was going to give her a kiss on the cheek and her pulse quickened. Jane caught her breath and looked into his beautiful blue eyes.

Instead of a kiss, he lightly squeezed her hand.

"It'll be fine. They're in love and have their whole lives ahead of them. The wedding will be gorgeous."

Jane felt his breath on her cheek, and she absorbed his strength and belief this evening would be magical.

As Jane entered the house from the back deck, Casey ran toward her with her hair in curlers and a panicked expression pinching her face. "Mom! There you are. Have you seen Vanessa?" Vanessa was the hairstylist and makeup artist.

"I'm here, sweetie." Vanessa swept into the room, and the three of them moved into the dressing area, aka the master suite.

"Oh, gosh, Mom, it just hit me that this is really real. I'm getting married. I'm about to become Drew's wife."

"Getting cold feet?" Vanessa asked. "'Cause you know you don't have to go through with this."

"Oh no, no. I adore Drew. I can't wait to be his wife. It's just that it's finally hitting me. This is forever."

"If you're lucky," Vanessa said. "It is."

"Mom?" Casey looked to her for reassurance, her voice sounding the way it did when she was a little girl and uncertain about something.

"Honey, this is all going to be perfect. And if it's

not perfect, you'll have an amazing story to tell of any hiccups, and that will be fine. I promise."

"I know. I'm sorry. It's like I'm a hot mess all of a sudden."

"All brides are hot messes just before the wedding," Vanessa said. "Trust me on this."

"I'm right here," Jane leaned over to kiss the top of her daughter's head. "If you need me for anything, I'm right by your side. No matter what."

✸✸✸✸✸✸✸✸✸✸✸✸✸

Later that afternoon, Jane helped Casey into her wedding gown. The delicate lace tea-length dress had cap sleeves and a scooped neckline that showed off Casey's elegant collarbone. The skirt was intricately embroidered with pearls and sequins that caught the light whenever she moved.

"You look absolutely stunning, sweetheart." Jane fastened an antique pearl necklace around Casey's neck. The pearls had been passed down from Jane's great-grandmother to Jane's mom to Jane and now to Casey.

"Thanks, Mom." Casey turned to give her a hug. "I'm so glad you're here with me today."

Jane's throat tightened with heartfelt emotion. "I wouldn't miss it for the world."

She held Casey's arm as she stepped into her white satin heels, and then Jane pinned back a few loose blond curls and adjusted the veil in place. Casey's hair was swept back on one side with a jeweled comb and the sheer veil fell delicately across her shoulders.

"You are the most stunning bride I have ever seen." Jane put a hand to her heart and let out a sigh of joy.

Casey beamed, her blue eyes shining. "I feel like a princess."

A knock sounded on the door. "Ten minutes till showtime," Trevor called.

Casey's smile faltered slightly. "I can't believe this is really happening. I'm getting married!"

Jane gave her daughter's shoulder a gentle squeeze. "It's normal to feel nervous. But I see the way you and Drew look at each other. This love is real."

Reassured, Casey nodded. "I've never been surer of anything in my life. I'm ready to walk down that aisle."

Arm in arm, they headed outside to the deck where Jane's father waited to escort Casey down the aisle. He gave a low whistle when he saw his granddaughter.

"Look at you, just as stunning as your mother on her wedding day," he said in his gravelly voice and offered Casey his arm. "Shall we?"

Jane kissed Casey's cheek. "See you out there. I love you."

Then she hurried down the stairs door to the beach to where white folding chairs were arranged in two sections, leaving a wide aisle down the center strewn with pale-pink rose petals. At the end of the aisle stood an arch woven from willow branches and decorated with flowers, seashells, and battery-powered twinkle lights.

Beyond the chairs, the sun sank low in the sky, casting a peachy glow across the water. The tide was going out, leaving a long stretch of flat, damp sand studded with tiny coquina shells as if perfectly placed by God. Gentle waves lapped at the shore. It was a breathtaking scene.

Trevor stood at the front as best man in a navy suit and tie, looking refined yet relaxed. Beside him, Drew kept shifting his weight and tugging at his collar, plainly nervous. Trevor leaned over to whisper something to Drew who broke into a smile and settled down.

Once all the guests were seated, the officiant nodded to the violinist who began playing the processional song, Pachelbel's "Canon in D." Jane's heart swelled as she watched her daughter step gracefully down the rose petal-strewn aisle on her grandfather's arm.

Casey's eyes were locked on Drew, her smile growing wider with each step closer. Drew's expression mirrored Casey's, as if he couldn't believe this vision gliding toward him was real. His look of pure love and amazement made Jane's breath catch.

Casey's grandfather placed her hand in Drew's before going to sit beside Jane's mother in the front row. Drew's hands trembled as he took Casey's, and she gave his fingers a reassuring squeeze.

"Welcome everyone," began the officiant. "We're gathered here today to celebrate the union of Casey and Drew, two special souls who found each other and discovered they were destined for lifelong love."

The officiant spoke about the blessings of marriage and read an excerpt from the Bible centered on true love, and then it was time for the vows.

Drew cleared his throat and blinked back happy tears. "Casey, the moment I first saw you, I felt something shift inside me. In your eyes, I found a twin flame to my soul that lit me up in a way I'd never known."

Casey's eyes were wet with happy tears.

Drew continued, his voice husky with emotion. "You helped me understand the random pieces of my life were leading me to you. My friend, my love, my partner—you are the missing piece of my soul. With you by my side, I know we can weather anything."

Casey dabbed at her eyes with a lace hand-kerchief.

"I promise to walk all of life's paths with you," Drew went on. "To be your strength when you are weary, your comfort when you despair, and your greatest fan when you soar. I vow to love you uncon-ditionally and create a home filled with joy, laughter, and light. You are my always and forever."

He slipped the ring onto her finger. By now, there wasn't a dry eye among the guests. Jane glanced at Trevor and saw him discreetly wipe his cheek with a knuckle. She teared up too. The officiant invited Casey to share her vows. Beaming at Drew, she began. "From our very first date, I felt I could tell you anything. Your patience and kindness healed my heart where it had been broken."

She smiled through happy tears. "When we're

together, the rest of the world fades away, and I know I'm safe in your arms. You see my soul when others only notice the surface."

Jane locked eyes with Trevor. He gave her a tender smile that took her breath away.

Casey's voice grew thicker with emotion. "You make me feel treasured beyond measure. I vow to cherish you just the same and create a peaceful haven where we nourish each other's dreams."

Trevor put his fingers to his lips and lightly blew Jane a kiss. She pretended to catch it and pressed her own fingertips to her mouth.

Turning Drew's hand palm up, Casey traced a heart onto his skin. "My heart is, and will always be, yours. In sunshine and rain, calm and trial, I will stand dutifully by your side as your faithful partner for all our days."

Sliding the ring onto his finger, she brought his hand to her lips for a tender kiss as more tears slipped down her cheeks.

After a short silence to allow the poignant words to resonate, the officiant said, "By the power vested in me by the State of Louisiana, I now pronounce you husband and wife. You may kiss your bride!"

Joyfully, Drew cradled Casey's face in both hands and kissed her as their family and friends broke into raucous applause. Laughing, Casey wrapped her arms around his neck, and they got lost in each other.

When they finally parted, the officiant presented them to the gathered guests. "It is my honor to introduce Mr. and Mrs. Drew Gardner!"

The newlyweds practically floated back up the petal-strewn aisle, faces alight with happiness. They accepted hugs and congratulations from guests along the way.

Trevor came to stand beside Jane and shook his son's hand, then enfolded Casey into a warm embrace.

"Welcome to the family," he said, choking up. "I wish you both a lifetime of love."

Jane hugged them next, tears of pride and joy slipping down her cheeks. She took Casey's face gently in her hands. "I'm so proud of the woman you've become. Your dad would be too."

"Thank you, Mom," Casey said, "I love you so much."

"I love you too, sweetie. More than you can know."

The rest of the guests followed the couple up the beach onto the deck where the reception would take place. Jane and Trevor held back, walking side by side.

"Can you believe our kids are married and just in time for Christmas?" Trevor asked, shaking his head in wonder.

"It seems like just yesterday I was dropping Casey off for her first day of kindergarten." Jane sighed wistfully. "Where does the time go?"

Trevor reached for her. "Before we know it, we could be grandparents."

Jane laughed. "Let's not rush things! For now, I'm just thrilled to see them so happy."

"Me too. Casey is a wonderful young woman and couldn't have picked anyone better for my son." Pride shone in Trevor's eyes.

"They're off to a beautiful start," Jane said, gazing out at the sun setting over the glittering water. "I know their love will last forever."

Trevor tipped her chin up to face him. "Like ours will also, this time around?"

Jane caught her breath and held his earnest gaze. The last of the sun's rays gilded his blond hair and deepened the smile lines around his eyes. Her heart swelled, all doubts vanishing.

"Yes," she said, "our forever starts today."

Trevor lowered his mouth to hers in a slow, tender kiss. The sounds of the sea and celebration faded away. In that perfect moment, nothing else mattered but love.

Arm in arm, they walked up the deck steps together, ready to join the reception and toast their children's future, which looked as bright and hopeful as their own rediscovered happily ever after.

THIRTEEN

Christmas

Beach

After the best reception ever, Drew and Casey retreated to a honeymoon suite at one of the local B&Bs. Jason headed back to New Orleans. The rest of the guests retreated to their own accommodations, leaving just Trevor and Jane at the beach house.

They worked until midnight tidying and packing up the place, which thankfully wasn't too big of a job since Suzy had stayed on top of cleanup during the reception.

Once everyone had left, and their bags were packed to head back to New Orleans in the morning to celebrate Christmas, Trevor turned to Jane. Moonlight streamed through the window, lining her delicate features in silver light.

"What an amazing wedding," Trevor said, drawing her into his arms. "But I barely got any time with you."

Jane settled her hands at his waist, thrilling at his nearness. "It was a whirlwind. But I wouldn't change a thing. It couldn't have gone better."

Trevor reached up to tuck a loose strand of hair behind her ear. "You're right."

Their eyes met and held, the air thickening between them. Ever so slowly, Trevor dipped his mouth to hers in a kiss that started soft and exploratory but quickly deepened into passionate urgency.

Trevor rested his forehead against Jane's. "Will you be with me tonight?"

Joy surged through Jane's veins. She trailed her fingers down his chest. "I thought you'd never ask."

With hands clasped, Trevor led her to the bedroom they'd shared when they were young. He paused outside the door to kiss Jane gently. "I've waited so long for this chance to love you again."

Jane's eyes misted. "I'm here now, my darling. I'm yours."

Trevor swept her into his arms and carried her over the threshold. Laying Jane tenderly across the bed, he stretched out beside her. Their mouths met again in eager kisses as hands roamed and bodies intertwined.

Outside, the ocean rumbled timelessly. Inside, soft sighs and murmurs filled the darkness as Trevor and Jane explored this new intimacy.

And at long last, their broken hearts were made whole in each other's arms.

****

On Christmas morning, pale winter light filtered through the sheer curtains of the beach house bedroom, rousing Jane from sleep. She blinked awake slowly, a smile spreading across her face.

Beside her, Trevor stirred and reached for her hand. His thumb stroked across her knuckles.

"Merry Christmas, my love," he murmured, his voice deep with drowsiness.

Jane rolled to face him, snuggling into his warm chest. "Merry Christmas," she said, thrilled at waking up in his arms. She placed a soft kiss over his heart.

Trevor tipped her chin up to claim her mouth in a slow, lingering kiss. Then he tucked a strand of hair behind her ear. "I can't imagine a better gift than having you here with me."

Jane's eyes misted. "You're the best gift ever."

They held each other in the quiet of the beach house, listening to the soothing rumble of waves outside. After all the years apart, and the misunderstandings between them, this felt like a miracle.

Trevor trailed his fingers idly up and down her arm. "We should start thinking about heading back soon. People will be expecting Christmas dinner."

Jane snuggled closer into his chest. "Mmm, five more minutes."

Chuckling, Trevor kissed the top of her head. "Whatever you want, my love."

Eventually, they slipped from bed to share a pot of coffee and toast with jam. Working in tandem, they tidied and locked up the beach house. Loading their bags into his truck, they set off toward New Orleans.

Jane curled up against Trevor's shoulder during the drive, perfectly content. The radio played classic Christmas carols as the countryside rolled by.

By late morning, they pulled up in front of Jane's cozy home, decorated merrily for the season. Casey and Drew were inside, beating them there. Soon, everyone else arrived—grandparents, Aunt Julie and her family with Henry, Suzy. The house was crowded and filled with laughter, just the way Jane liked it.

Casey was married. Jane's little girl was a wife now. It seemed unreal. And to Drew, Trevor's son, of all people.

What were the odds?

Jane allowed herself a moment of bittersweet nostalgia for the past. If only David could have lived to see this day...

But life moved on, and Jane had so much to be grateful for.

The kitchen was packed as everyone pitched in to prepare food and put dinner on the table. Jane was making prime rib. Casey turned on Christmas music and Bing Crosby filled the house. Suzy poured mulled wine and eggnog for anyone who wanted something festive to drink. They laughed and told stories and had the best time.

At one point, Trevor slipped into the kitchen

and discreetly touched Jane's arm. "Excuse us a moment," he said to the others, and guided Jane out to the deserted hallway.

"What is it?" she asked.

"I have a present I wanted to give you in private," he said, eyes twinkling. "Before the wrapping paper starts flying and things get lost in the shuffle."

He passed her a white present wrapped in red ribbon. She unwrapped it and opened the box, then she opened the inside box to reveal a glittering star-shaped pendant.

"It's beautiful." She exhaled.

"It was supposed to be your Christmas present the year we broke up," he said.

She glanced up at him, tears filming her eyes. "You kept it all these years?"

"Yeah."

"Why?"

"At first I was certain we'd get back together. I stuck it in my safe deposit box, and then I just forgot it was there until we started dating again. It made me think of that night we first kissed on Christmas Beach all those years ago. Remember? We were gazing at the stars, and you said you wished on the first star you saw."

Jane's throat tightened at the poignant memory. "I did get my wish that night," she whispered. "You."

Trevor caressed her cheek, his blue eyes full of emotion. "And now I'm yours again, for good this time. We're writing our own happy ending."

He clasped the necklace gently around her neck.

Overwhelmed with love, Jane pulled him into a lingering kiss.

When they finally eased apart, Trevor kept her in his arms. "There's something else I need to tell you."

"Oh?"

"I've been in talks with the hospital to move my practice to New Orleans in the new year."

Jane's eyes widened. "Really?"

"Really." He tucked a loose strand of hair behind her ear. "If you will have me, I want to be closer to you."

Joy surged through Jane's heart. "Of course! That would be a dream come true."

They stood wrapped in each other, foreheads touching. From the kitchen came the sound of laughter and the family singing off-key Christmas carols.

"I love you, Jane," Trevor whispered. "Now and always."

"I love you too," Jane said. "This is the happiest Christmas ever."

Their tender kiss lingered sweetly until the kids' excited voices called them back to share in more Christmas magic.

Hand in hand, Jane and Trevor joined their family, ready to celebrate their new beginning.

EPILOGUE

One year later...

Christmas Eve on the Louisiana coast was mild and clear. Twinkling lights lined the beach house deck as the sun sunk low over the glittering ocean. Inside, Jane admired her reflection in the mirror.

Her ivory lace gown was simple, yet elegant. Jane twisted her hair into a low bun and secured it with a pearl comb. Tonight, surrounded by loved ones, she would finally marry her first love, Trevor.

A soft knock sounded. "Come in," Jane called.

The door opened and Casey entered, positively glowing in a red holiday dress that skimmed her gentle baby bump. Jane's heart swelled at the sight. She could hardly believe her little girl was about to become a mother herself!

"You look amazing, Mom." Casey squeezed Jane's hand. "Dad would be so happy for you."

Jane's eyes misted. "I hope so. I wish he could be here for his first grandchild, but I know he's watching over us." She took a steadying breath. "Shall we?"

Arm in arm, they made their way downstairs where Trevor waited on the beach with the officiant. Candles flickered along the willow aisle. A violinist played soft music as Jane glided across the sand to Trevor.

His eyes shone with wonder when he saw her, just as they had the first time all those years ago. Jane barely heard the officiant speak, lost in Trevor's loving gaze.

A few minutes later, he was sliding a ring onto her finger and kissing her tenderly to joyous applause.

At long last, they were husband and wife.

✦∗✦∗✦∗✦∗✦∗✦∗✦∗

Dear Reader,

Thank you so much for reading *Christmas Beach*. If you enjoyed Trevor and Jane's story, we would so appreciate a review! You have no idea how much it means to us! Readers rock our world.

Please look out for the second book in the *Christmas Beach series, Christmas Beach Proposal*.

You can visit Susan on her website @ https://susansands.com/.

If you'd like to keep up with Lori's latest releases, you can visit her on the web @ www.loriwilde.com.

Much love and light!

—Lori and Susan

About the Authors

Susan Sands pulls her stories from the very Southern settings where she grew up in rural Louisiana. She is the published author of nine full-length Southern romantic novels and four novellas. Her tenth novel will be released by Tule Publishing in May of 2024.

★☆★☆★☆★☆★☆★

Lori Wilde is the New York Times, USA Today and Publishers' Weekly bestselling author of 99 works of fiction. She's a three time Romance Writers' of America RITA finalist and has four times been nominated for Romantic Times Readers' Choice

Award. She has won numerous other awards as well and five million of her books are in print. Her *Wedding Veil Wishes* series has inspired six movies from Hallmark and her breakout book, *The First Love Cookie Club* was filmed by Hallmark as *A Kismet Christmas*.

f X ⊙

Also by Lori Wilde

CHRISTMAS BEACH

Christmas Beach Wedding

Christmas Beach Proposal

Christmas Beach Reunion

KRINGLE, TEXAS

A Perfect Christmas Gift

A Perfect Christmas Wish

A Perfect Christmas Surprise

A Perfect Christmas Joy

A Perfect Christmas Reunion

A Perfect Christmas Kiss

TEXAS RASCALS SERIES

Keegan

Matt

Nick

Kurt

Tucker

Kael

Truman

Dan

Rex

Clay

Jonah